# "Why did you think this house would appeal to me?"

All the amusement had left Luke's voice as he asked the question. He was deadly serious now.

"I don't know," she answered unsteadily, caught off guard.

"I think you do," he said, regarding her with unwelcome directness. "It reminded you of the farmhouse at Tarsac."

"No," she denied hotly. "That's not what I thought. Why should it even have entered my head?"

But had it—subconsciously, at least? He was still looking at her with that quiet intentness that made her want to look away, but she didn't dare. She was held captive.

"Because you're hung up on the idea of the man I was then," he said. "Put it out of your mind, Amber. I'm not that man. Any more than you are that girl."

D0047600

**Lee Stafford** was born and educated in Sheffield where she worked as a secretary and in public relations. Her husband is in hospital catering management. They live in Sussex with their two teenage daughters.

## Books by Lee Stafford

HARLEQUIN ROMANCE
2963—YESTERDAY'S ENEMY

Don't miss any of our special offers. Write to us at the following address for information on our newest releases.

Harlequin Reader Service
901 Fuhrmann Blvd., P.O. Box 1397, Buffalo, NY 14240
Canadian address: P.O. Box 603,
Fort Erie, Ont. L2A 5X3

# A Song
# in the Wilderness

## Lee Stafford

# Harlequin Books

TORONTO • NEW YORK • LONDON
AMSTERDAM • PARIS • SYDNEY • HAMBURG
STOCKHOLM • ATHENS • TOKYO • MILAN

Original hardcover edition published in 1989
by Mills & Boon Limited

ISBN 0-373-03048-7

Harlequin Romance first edition April 1990

# CHAPTER ONE

AMBER was in her office in the Faculty of Arts, waiting in awful anticipation for the telephone on her desk to ring, announcing Lucas Tremayne's arrival. As she went about her morning tasks, opening and sorting mail and organising the papers Professor Doyle would need to take to his various committees, the sense of dread built up, darkening the bright spring morning like a doomy cloud. She kept glancing at the phone nervously, expecting any moment the summons from the porter's lodge which meant she must go down and conduct the new member of staff through the labyrinthine corridors of the old university building.

Ring, damn you! She glared at the instrument balefully, anxious now to have the ordeal of this meeting over with. A brief scan of her newspaper over breakfast had told her that it was, for once, a quiet day in the world's trouble spots. There was no catastrophe which would claim the prior attention of this eminent journalist and allow her to postpone or avoid the moment she so feared. He would be here, and she would have to face him.

'Good morning. I'm either in the Department of English or I'm hopelessly lost.'

Amber froze. She had been waiting with such intense concentration for the shrill of the telephone that she had not heard the click of the door opening behind her. But she knew that voice, the dry, understated timbre which contrasted so oddly with its owner's restless, vibrating energy. It hadn't changed, but in that moment before she was obliged to turn round, Amber hoped that Lucas Tremayne had. Maliciously, she wished that the photo on the dust-jacket of his best-seller was an old one, that his hair had thinned and his waistline thickened—after all, he must be pushing forty!

For if *he* had changed, so must she, from the breathless teenager she had been when they last met. She was twenty-eight, now—perhaps, she hoped despairingly, he would not recognise her.

'Mr Tremayne?' She faced him, putting on an impersonal smile. 'It's a wonder you aren't lost. The porter was supposed to ring through and let me know you had arrived.'

It was unfair, unfair! The years had done little, essentially, to alter Luke Tremayne, beyond adding a few more fascinating lines of character to a face tanned and freckled by frequent exposure to hostile foreign skies. There was no obvious grey in the thick thatch of sun-bleached, reddish-blond hair which retained its tendency to flop over his forehead. The mouth still bore that odd quality of bittersweet humour, offset by a certain pugnacity of jaw that testified to his capacity for forcefulness.

'He was talking to someone, so I just wandered up on my own.' He shrugged and smiled, the same crooked, irreverent grin that assaulted his readers from the flyleaf of *When the Guns are Silent*, his much-acclaimed novel of Middle-Eastern war and drama. She blinked, looked down, looked up again and caught him regarding her with the faintest of question marks in eyes which were dazzlingly blue under strongly defined brows.

'I don't believe it!' he said softly. 'It's you!'

Amber found herself incapable of speech. Of course she hadn't seriously thought he would fail to know her, but she was still stunned by the reality of this man who was so nearly the Luke she remembered. The spare, ahtletic body had not gained so much as an ounce, she could see that, even though it was at present confined in a sports jacket and casual trousers. He was built for action, with a compact, dense, powerful musculature that would have made him an ideal squash or tennis international, and he looked more like a soldier of fortune in some mercenary army...as he had once, indeed, been...than a man of letters.

Her silence lengthened, and his laugh was a little short.

'Oh, come off it!' he exclaimed. 'Are we playing charades, or what? It's hardly conceit to assume you remember me, and no man would fail to recognise a woman he had known in such intimate circumstances!'

Angered by his brazen reference to something she would have preferred not to have mentioned, she said tartly, 'He might if he had known as many, since then, as the gossip columns of certain newspapers credit him with!'

'Ah.' He shook his head ruefully. 'It's difficult, but journalistic training sharpens the memory. France, wasn't it? Ten, maybe almost eleven years ago? You had a hired bike and a sweet nature, both of which you seem to have dispensed with along the way.'

He was teasing her, that much was obvious, and it was all Amber could do not to explode with resentment. She was deeply embarrassed, too, by the way his eyes reconnoitred her, reminding her of that

passionate afternoon long ago, and her own in-
genuous, unhesitant response. She saw him lying flat
on his back in the jungle-garden at Tarsac, saw him
smiling down at her compassionately as she sat, hot
and dust-streaked on a café terrace in a small *bastide*
town. And by the pool, with the sunlight reflecting
water, and the shadows from the trees striping his
powerful shoulders with bars of variegated golden
light.

She inhaled deeply. Now was the moment. She had
to do it, although it galled her to ask any favours of
him when he seemed to derive so much amusement
from what, to her, were painful recollections.

'As you say, that was all a long time ago,' she said.
'It has nothing to do with my present life—or yours.
In fact, I'd prefer it if you said nothing about it to
anyone.'

He appeared to consider this.

'Fair enough. I don't usually kiss and tell, in spite
of those aforementioned articles in the popular Press.
There *are* ladies who aren't so modest, and so-called
journalists who don't trouble to check their sources.
You needn't worry, Amber.' The clearly etched brows
arched a little higher. 'A distinctive, unusual name
like that would be an automatic memory-jogger, even
if the rest of you were forgettable. But as far as the
University of Westbury is concerned, you and I were
no more than passing acquaintances.'

Even if the rest of you were forgettable! Amber
burned at that remark, surmising that her youthful,
inexperienced loving had been exactly that to this man
who was obviously a connoisseur of women.

'As far as the University of Westbury is concerned,
you and I have never met before!' she snapped. Her

all too ready temper subsiding a little, she went on, 'Don't you see, it's easier that way? It avoids the necessity for explanations. After all, you will only be here for a term.'

He smiled knowingly. 'And you haven't told any of your colleagues that we had a prior acquaintance? Then I suppose I had better play the gentleman and go along with this fiction. Otherwise you're going to feel rather foolish, aren't you? I hope you're suitably grateful for my complicity.'

Amber was incapable of anything so mild as gratitude. She was choking inwardly with rage, anger at him because his coming here had put her in this odious position, and at herself because she felt the need for this ridiculous subterfuge. What was more, she was sure he was aware of her suppressed fury, and beneath his mild amusement lay something else—a kind of puzzled insult. Perhaps he expected any female to be delighted to have her name linked sexually with his?

While she was still struggling for a reply, the door opened again, and the lean, grey, bespectacled figure of Professor Doyle appeared.

'Mr Tremayne!' he said warmly. 'Welcome to Westbury. I see my secretary, Mrs Kingsland, is taking care of you. She's the linchpin of the department, and if you have any problems, there are few she can't solve.'

The professor was strong on formality. Amber had worked for him for three years, and he still addressed her as 'Mrs Kingsland'. Right now, she wished it were not so, because his words had caused Luke to glance swiftly at the narrow gold circlet on the third finger of her left hand. And, looking up at her face again, his own expression said plainly, I see. But he didn't, of course, and it was impossible to tell him he'd got hold of the wrong end of the stick.

She turned to the professor, taking refuge in the everyday business of the university.

'The Senate papers are already on your desk, Professor Doyle. And Professor Hudson from History asked if you would chair the faculty meeting next Tuesday. I've pencilled it in your diary, since you appear to be free, but if you'd like me to make your excuses...'

He groaned, glacing up at the ceiling as if in supplication.

'No, I had better do it. It *is* my turn.' To the younger man, he said, 'Once one becomes a head of department, administration outweighs both teaching and research, I'm afraid. One deplores it, but is caught in the trap.'

Lucas Tremayne laughed. Amber caught the echoes of recklessness in that laughter, but some of the frenetic, live-for-today carelessness she remembered had gone. Time must have touched him in some ways.

'You have my sympathy. Even the copy-room at the *Examiner* frightens the hell out of me,' he confessed. 'As for the editor's office—that much permanence I'm not ready for!'

Amber, who was in no position to profess such breezy independence, battled with a deep groundswell of resentment. These brave spirits who resisted shackles usually preserved their freedom at someone else's expense, she thought bitterly.

'If that's the case, I'm surprised you've come to Westbury,' she heard herself interjecting tartly. 'Aren't you afraid university life will tie you down? We don't get much excitement here—for a man who's used to being in the hot spots.'

His eyes lingered thoughtfully on her, taking in the piquantly distinctive, almost triangular face, with its neat little chin and green, slanted eyes, the mahogany-coloured hair cut in layers of varying length, feathering about it. The observant watchfulness hardened as he continued to stare, sending a sudden chill down her spine.

'That's a temporary arrangement. I'm committed only to giving a series of lectures over a period of one term,' he reminded her. 'Even I need a break from excitement now and then. But you'll scarcely know I'm here, Mrs Kingsland. I'm just passing through.'

Aren't you always? she thought wryly, biting her lip to prevent the retort from slipping out.

Professor Doyle glanced enquiringly at his secretary. She was resourceful and normally unflappable, and put in more work on her part-time basis than many of the nine-to-fivers, but a formidable temper went with those auburn locks. He wasn't sure why, but he could tell from the mutinous set of her chin, and the tautening of her lips, that it was simmering away now.

'See if you can track down Dr Courtney for me,' he suggested gently. 'I know he's looking forward to meeting Mr Tremayne, but you know how he is. He's probably in the library.'

Where he's got involved in some research and lost all sense of time, Amber thought affectionately, her humour returning.

'I'll find him. Coffee for . . . five, then? I expect Dr Barnes and Dr Dreiser will be joining you?'

'I can see you have a pearl beyond price here, Professor,' Lucas Tremayne remarked languidly.

'Absolutely,' beamed Professor Doyle, completely missing the taunting note in the other man's voice, Amber was sure. 'How we ever managed without her to organise us, I'll never know.'

Amber, already dialling, resisted the urge to hurl the telephone at the pair of them. They were both patronising her; the professor innocently and meaning well—he had the *naïveté* about more worldly matters common to many academics, brilliant in their own specialities. Lucas Tremayne, on the other hand, was very gently but deliberately sneering at her.

I'm not just an efficient machine that makes coffee and arrangements and types papers, nor am I a dim-witted ninny who throws herself into the arms of men she hardly knows, she wanted to scream. I have dreams and ambitions, *and* a brain, and a life that takes place outside these walls. Don't diminish me with praise, or denigrate me with smart-alec wit!

She was still seething as the door closed behind them. A whole term! It was only a few short months, but how was she to survive them, find a way of dealing with the unwanted presence of Luke Tremayne back in her life, uninvited, after so long?

*You'll scarcely know I'm here.*

She would know. He was too forceful, too extrovert, too charismatic not to make himself felt. He'd be there, in the office, in the corridors, in the common-room. His charm would seduce everyone into liking him, despite—or perhaps because of—his reputation. The students would all adore him, and he'd be an instant cachet at all the at-homes and sherry parties.

It had been decided some time ago that the department would employ a writer-in-residence to enhance the creative-writing course, but the original choice for this position, an elderly poet, had unfortunately died during the winter. Since a re-think had been forced on them, Calvin Dreiser, the youthful American lecturer, had suggested they invite someone younger, more contemporary, with whom the students could identify.

'By that, I expect you mean some whiz-kid from Yale or Harvard, who's unknown this side of the Atlantic?' Sorrel Barnes demanded scathingly.

They were in the pub where university personnel congregated, and Sorrel tapped the rim of her glass with an immaculate, plum-coloured fingernail, her other hand smoothing the linen skirt over her shapely knees. Amber smiled into her drink. Those two were forever sniping at each other. Sorrel was smart, brilliant and fashionable, and resented the fact that Cal refused to be impressed by her.

Instinctively, they all turned to Gerald Courtney, as the senior member of staff present. His bushy moustache twitched as he pursued a lemon pip around his gin and tonic with a cocktail stick, and no one worried when he didn't pronounce judgement immediately.

'It would need to be someone with sufficient literary merit, experience and authority to be an asset to the course,' he pointed out, at length. They bandied names around the table for a while, no one finding it odd when Amber joined in. Although she worked as a secretary, her background was solidly academic, and her views were usually accorded consideration.

It was Cal who dropped the bombshell.

'What about that reporter guy who's always in the front line wherever a war's going on? The one who wrote that novel which scooped all the literary prizes and was made into a film? You must have seen it, Gerald.'

'I never go to the cinema,' Gerald Courtney said loftily. 'I don't care for sharing my intellectual pleasures with a dark auditorium full of sweaty bodies. However, I did read the book. It was both thought-provoking and dramatic—marvellously written. What *is* the fellow's name?'

'Tremayne.' Sorrel sipped fastidiously at her Campari and soda. 'Lucas Tremayne. I saw him being interviewed on television not long ago. He had the interviewer tied up in verbal knots in no time. He'd make a terrific lecturer. But he's just come back from America having made a fortune out of that film. He's working on another book, so it's said, and still writing his foreign column for the *Examiner*. Why on earth should he want to come to Westbury? You're off your rails, Cal, as usual.'

They were all so fiercely involved in this discussion that none of them noticed Amber was gripping her glass so tightly that her knuckles were white. Her face was a carefully controlled rictus of protest.

'He's far too famous and important to consider it,' she said quickly. 'What's more, he's hardly the right person to be lecturing to impressionable undergraduates. His entire life reads like one of those novels with flamboyant dust-jackets that one buys on station platforms. Kicked out of public school for some misdemeanour involving girls. Fighting in some African guerrilla leader's private army. Marrying a photographer whose life-style was as dubious as his own, taking her with him into a war zone, where she was killed, then in and out of innumerable beds before her body was even cold——' Her voice faltered, choking with a disgust she realised sounded far too personal, and she restrained herself with difficulty. 'I just don't think it's fitting,' she finished lamely.

'Why, Amber!' Cal looked at her in surprise, running a hand through his short-cropped brown hair. 'It isn't like you to be prudish. The guy's led a colourful life—so what? It's made him one hell of a writer.'

'I'm surprised you read all that gossip column nonsense, Amber, let alone believe it,' Sorrel remarked lightly.

'There isn't usually smoke without fire,' Amber contended stubbornly. 'Prof probably won't buy the idea, anyhow,' she added, brightening with relief and wondering why she was getting paranoid over a suggestion the head of department would probably veto. Lucas Tremayne was a wild card, a maverick. The professor was conservative enough to distrust a man with so bizarre a reputation. It would all come to nothing.

But she had forgotten that the staid, contemplative life of the university had always held a place for the strange, the contentious, the eccentric—and the downright revolutionary. Professor Doyle was sufficiently impressed by Lucas Tremayne's literary prowess and achievements to give the idea serious consideration, and was intrigued by his secretary's less than enthusiastic attitude.

'Amber thinks Tremayne will seduce all the female undergraduates, and have the guys all wrapping tea-towels round their heads and rushing off to join the

Foreign Legion,' Cal said irreverently, and the green eyes favoured him with a frosty glare.

'Stranger things have happened,' she retorted darkly. 'That may be a slight exaggeration, but I *do* feel he would be a disturbing influence.'

'My dear young lady, part of the reason for coming to university is to be disturbed,' the professor pointed out gently. 'To have one's ideas shaken up, not merely confirmed, by an inspiring, original lecturer who sees the world from a different angle. Perhaps Mr Tremayne would provide the spice of unorthodoxy—the seasoning all dishes require.'

'Too much pepper makes food unpalatable,' Amber declared, unimpressed by the culinary metaphor. 'Anyhow, he won't come. Why should he? Certainly he doesn't need the money—the proceeds from that film must have made him as rich as Croesus.'

But she was wrong. Mr Tremayne replied to the letter of invitation she was obliged to draft that he would be delighted to do a term as writer in residence at Westbury—with the proviso that he was still retained by the *Examiner* and, should a really important foreign news story break, the paper would have prior claim on him.

There was nothing Amber could do, as the weeks passed and arrangements were made for his arrival. She could hardly say to her employer, Please don't bring this man here, because once, long ago, he broke my heart, and I have good reasons for keeping him out of my life.

The more she thought about it, the more sure in her mind she became that she did not want anyone at Westbury to know about what had happened between herself and Lucas Tremayne. It was vital that she maintained a distance between them, and that distance depended on divorcing the past from the present.

She kept herself furiously busy that morning, while Luke was closeted with the professor and the other members of staff, presumably discussing the details of the course. But somehow she knew it was too much to hope that she would not be obliged to face him again, and just before twelve-thirty he came into her office, alone, and closed the door carefully behind him.

Amber wasn't sure whether she was thankful for the privacy this ensured them, or half afraid of the unwelcome intimacy.

'Is there something I can do for you, Mr Tremayne?' she enquired coolly.

He laughed shortly.

'You could call me Luke, as you did before. Everyone else already does, apart from the professor. Otherwise it's going to seem rather strange,' he pointed out. 'Apart from that, no, thank you. I don't require your assistance—yet. I just wanted to say that I grasped the reason for your insistence on secrecy when I learned you were married. Silly of me—I should have realised that you would be by now.'

Amber had been standing by the filing cabinet when he'd come in, and she had not moved, but remained frozen there, like a statue. He came closer, leaning one elbow on the cabinet top, and regarding her with a questioning, slightly humorous gaze.

'A bit much, though, isn't it?' he demanded lightly. 'I mean—no one is that pure nowadays, or expects anyone else to be. Did your husband imagine he'd married a virgin? If so, he won't find out about your past adventures from me.'

Adventures? One afternoon of careless but memorable lovemaking, Amber thought ruefully. But her amatory experiences—or lack of them—were none of his business.

'My husband is dead,' she said curtly. 'He was killed in a road accident five years ago.'

She thought the blue eyes softened a little, but his sympathy only made her more wary of him.

'I'm sorry,' he said. 'The professor referred to you as Mrs Kingsland, and our modern western society doesn't have a more precise means of expressing status. But it must have been hard for you. I know— I lost my wife tragically, too.'

So tragically that you lost no time in seeking consolation, she would have liked to retort. Whereas in her own case there had been no one else since Lawrence died. Her bed had been empty, the sensual side of her nature locked in on itself.

But even as the accusation formed in her mind, she knew that she could not lay claim to superior virtue or inconsolable grief. Had she ever really loved Lawrence in that way, so that her body ached at nights for the lack of him? It had not been that way, she knew. And over the last five years, she had simply closed a door on that part of her womanhood. There had been quite enough to cope with as it was, and to be truthful she had not really missed it. It was in many ways a relief to climb into bed alone, without having to surrender to demands she could not meet.

'And you haven't remarried,' she said. It was a statement, not a question. His publicity was accessible enough.

'I've rarely been in one place long enough to make it a sensible proposition,' he said. 'Added to the indisputable truth that I'm not the stuff good husbands are made of. Do you have any kids?'

'Just one daughter, Kate.'

Amber came to life and began putting the confidential files away, as she always did before going to lunch. She wished he would leave.

'Kate, short for Katherine? How old is she?'

She slammed the cabinet shut, turned the key in the lock.

'She's nine. Not that it's any business of yours,' she said heavily.

'Not that it is,' he agreed equably. 'Asking questions is a habit of mine. The answers usually help build up a picture, and the one I'm getting is of a young lady mighty anxious to rush to the altar. You certainly didn't waste any time. It must have been very soon after we . . . met.'

'That's right. I told you there was someone,' she said firmly.

'So you did. You also told me about your literary ambitions. You wanted to be a writer.'

Amber looked down, the swinging, feathery mass of her hair concealing her profile.

'Right now, I want to go for my lunch,' she told him decisively. 'So if we can conclude the interview——'

She was never so thankful for anything as she was for Cal's interruption then.

'We're off down the pub now—you said you'd join us, Luke,' he said cheerfully. 'Coming, Amber?'

She shook her head.

'Sorry, Cal. I can't make it. I have to shop for new jodhpurs for Kate.'

'That won't take up all your lunch hour, surely?' he objected.

'Yes, it will,' Amber insisted irritably. 'I need to shop around and compare prices. Have you *tried* buying jodhpurs lately? They're ruinously expensive.'

'Honey, my interest in gee-gees stops at Newmarket and Epsom,' Cal grinned. 'You should get that kid of yours interested in something less hazardous—like embroidery, or country dancing.'

'I should be so lucky!' Amber muttered, and somehow she could not avoid glancing in Luke's direction. He gave her the blandest of smiles.

'Sorry you can't come—Amber,' he said, trying out her name as if it were the first time he'd used it. 'And thanks for your...er...help.'

To her utter chagrin, while his back was turned to Cal, he actually winked at her.

She glared after his retreating back. He was determined to treat her request for discretion as some kind of joke, an amusing, slightly risqué secret they shared between them, and which he had condescended not to divulge to anyone else. She supposed, having promised her his silence, he would keep his word, but she would have to pay with nudges, winks and *double entendre* remarks. He would remind her in a hundred subtle ways of the things she had once allowed him...wanted him to do to her. Why? What did it matter to him, after so many years? Or did he just enjoy teasing anyone female?

She sighed as she picked up her handbag and shrugged on her jacket. The trouble was that even at this remove she could not, and never had been able to, make sense of what had happened to her on that long-ago summer in France. It all had a shimmering unreality, like a dream that had turned with startling rapidity into a nightmare.

One moment she had been an innocent girl, full of hopes and ambitions, tingling with anticipation of the wonderful future which lay ahead, golden and unexplored. Then she had met Luke, and all at once she had been grappling helplessly with adult emotions. Just as swiftly, it was over, and she was a woman alone, facing anguish, disillusion—and a deep dilemma.

The life she had made for herself since was different from the one she had planned, but she had lived it resolutely and determinedly, refusing to look back. The feelings she'd had for Luke Tremayne, and for no one else, she had pushed away, buried so deep that she thought she could never be called upon to examine them in the merciless glare of daylight. But they hadn't gone away, they were there, ticking ominously, like one of those long-buried wartime bombs which still had the dangerous potential to explode.

Amber bought the jodhpurs quickly. A seasoned shopper for expensive equestrian gear on a tight budget, she knew perfectly well where to find the best value. The excuse she had given Cal for missing the lunchtime rendezvous she would normally have kept was precisely that—an excuse.

But it was easy to see that she was very quickly going to run out of excuses which would keep her out of Luke Tremayne's way. Everyone was going to wonder just what game she was playing. He was going to wonder, too, and that sharp, investigative brain might come up with some likely answers, unless she was a lot cleverer about it than she had been today.

Because she had lied to him—consciously, deliberately, knowing full well the chance she was taking, but seeing no other way. And, having taken that step, she had to see it through, and somehow ensure that he did not find out.

# CHAPTER TWO

WHEN Amber got home to the cottage a few miles from Westbury where she lived with her daughter, there was no sign of Kate, and the place had the closed, empty look which declared that no one had been home since they had both left it that morning, she to go to work after dropping Kate off at the local village school.

Amber got out of the ancient Mini and slammed the door with unnecessary viciousness. Typical—Kate would be down at Lucy's stables again, and would come home happy, filthy, and redolent of horse manure, expecting an enormous meal to be on the table—as if potatoes peeled themselves, or salad leapt on to plates ready-washed!

She checked herself as she unlocked the door and let herself in. There was really no need to vent her bad temper on her absent daughter. It wasn't Kate's fault that the past had risen up to slap Amber in the face. And under normal circumstances a child of Kate's age would be coming back from school to a home with her mother already there, not an empty house and a list of chores.

If she didn't need the money so badly, Amber thought with a sigh. If she could afford to take six months or a year off, sit down and see if she could write as she had once been so confident she would. But it was too great a risk. She couldn't last that long without money coming in, even if success were guaranteed—which it wasn't. And if she gave up her job at the university, someone else would snap it up, and where else would she find compatible employment which fitted—well, almost—around her family life, among people she liked, and in an environment which suited her?

Amber pulled herself together and got to work on the dinner, after changing out of the skirt and jacket she wore for the office into faded jeans and an old checked sweatshirt. Her critical eye noted that the kitchen could do with a lick of paint, the pine cupboards and dresser needed sanding and re-varnishing, and it was time she ran up some new curtains to replace the present ones, which had seen better days.

And that was *before* she got around to the carpet in the living-room, which was worn in patches so she had to arrange the furniture to conceal them, and the three-piece suite which needed re-covering, still bearing the ravages of Kate's younger days and the attention of the cat which was now rubbing dedicatedly around her ankles.

Cash—it all came down to that! Would she ever have believed it, that long-ago summer when she'd not yet turned eighteen, passed her A-levels, and had the world at her feet, that her preoccupations would be carpets and cans of paint, and bills waiting to be paid?

The garden gate clicked, and her uncharacteristic mood of self-pity dissolved as she saw Kate strolling up the path. She had changed into the old clothes she kept down at Lucy's, and her school uniform would be screwed up and shoved into the bag she carried over her shoulder; it would need ironing, but would be at least clean and un-horsified, Amber thought with a grin, amazed, as she was every day, by how tall and how quickly her daughter was growing. Skinny and coltish, just as she herself had been at that age, her hair, a shade lighter than Amber's, scraped back and tied in a ponytail, riding hat swinging from one hand.

She's like me—isn't she? Amber asked herself. Well, yes, essentially her features resembled Amber's, except that her nose was more snub, less delicate, and she was blessed—or cursed—with freckles, which Amber never had. She shook her head involuntarily, and went back to shredding lettuce.

'Hi, Mum.' Kate dropped her bag unceremoniously on the kitchen floor, and flopped on to a chair. 'What a time I had! Beauty was in a pig of a mood—she backed me into the stable while I was trying to groom her, and I couldn't get out. Scarlet was playing up a bit as well—I don't know what's got into the horses today.'

There must be something going around, Amber thought grimly.

'Perhaps it's spring in the air,' she suggested, and then, with a slight frown, 'I know I said I wouldn't go on, but I hope you're careful around those horses.'

'I am. I know what I'm doing,' Kate declared confidently. 'Lucy taught me herself, and *she* trusts me. Don't worry, Mum.'

'OK.' Amber lit the grill and loaded chops and sausages on to it. 'Point taken. I know I'm turning into an old nag—if you'll pardon the pun.'

Kate had been involved with horses since Amber made friends with Lucy, who owned a riding stables, when she first came to live here in the early years of her marriage, and by now, she supposed, she should have stopped being nervous about the more dangerous aspects of equitation. Her daughter was a competent little rider, unafraid, and totally devoted to the animals, and it was obviously a love which was not going to lessen with the years. She mucked out, groomed, and generally helped around the stables, and in return Lucy cut the cost of Kate's own riding, for which Amber was realistic enough to be grateful.

Kate giggled now as she got up, washed her hands and began to lay the table.

'Don't be silly, Mum, you're not old. What you need is a boyfriend. Lucy says that's what's wrong with Beauty, now, she's——'

'All right, Kate, you don't need to go into detail,' Amber said hastily, thinking that she would have to have a word or two with Lucy! To look at her friend, slim, fair, and refined, one would never guess it, but horsey people had of necessity a basic earthiness, and Kate was already in the process of acquiring it. 'Beauty is one thing—I'm another, and our problems have nothing in common.'

She turned the sausages, which were in danger of burning.

'Lucy has a boyfriend. A new one,' Kate informed her sagaciously. 'He's there, now. His name's Tom, and he runs a stud farm.'

Back to sex again! Amber dished up the food and turned off the gas. A divorcee for longer than Amber had known her, Lucy took and discarded men cheerfully when the mood took her, as practical about her own needs as she was about her mares'. Amber had never been able to do that. Sex without total involvement didn't work for her—well, it hadn't with Lawrence, although she'd tried, truly she had. Sex with total involvement hadn't been an unqualified success, either, she recalled dourly. She'd given Luke all she had, willingly, the whole of her young, un-sullied heart and untouched body. He'd taken them lightly, carelessly, and tossed them aside.

'Well,' she said, 'that's a handy kind of boyfriend for Lucy to have. For the horses, I mean,' she added quickly. 'Ugh—Kate! Do you have to douse *every-thing* you eat in quite so much tomato sauce?'

'I like tomato sauce,' Kate said unworriedly, to which Amber, at that moment, could find no reasonable answer. She had a sudden wild yearning to cook a meal which wasn't eaten with one eye on the clock for the fastest getaway—an adult meal, with expensive ingredients like avocados and fresh prawns, and a bottle of good wine.

But it was pointless without an appreciative com-panion to share it, and Amber found herself recalling an unpretentious *auberge* in a sleepy village in the Dordogne. A 'chariot' of hors-d'oeuvres, tiny pieces of spicy sausage and seafood and raw vegetables. Fresh river trout cooked in white wine, shallots and cream. *Tarte aux abricots,* and an earthenware carafe of the house white.

'Simple French food at its best,' Luke had said. 'If it isn't available at the market that morning, *madame* doesn't buy it, and you won't find it on the menu.'

Why was it as clear in her memory, that meal, as if she had eaten it yesterday... the meal and the afternoon that followed it? Just because Luke was here, that was no excuse to keep dredging up the past. That was the last thing she must do. She might start sentimentalising it, seeing all the pain and humili-ation and bewilderment through a rosy, romantic filter, and that would be foolish.

'Can I go now?' Kate asked impatiently. 'I haven't any homework, and it will be light for ages.'

'Just as soon as we've washed up,' Amber said levelly, piling the dirty dishes into the sink. Kate grimaced, but grabbed the teatowel without complaint this time. They'd lived alone together for too long not to know when either of them was in earnest.

Kate was putting the cutlery noisily back into the drawer while Amber made herself coffee, when she happened to glance out of the kitchen window.

'Whose is that car outside, Mum?' she asked curiously. 'I didn't know anyone was coming. And we don't know anybody with a car as snobby as that!'

Amber switched off the kettle and joined her daughter at the window.

'That, my love, is a Jaguar,' she murmured. No wonder she hadn't heard it purring stealthily to a halt. And that, she added to herself, suddenly as cold as ice inside, is Luke Tremayne. What the hell was *he* doing here, uninvited? How dared he burst in on her at home like this?

'You can go out now, Kate,' she said, as casually as possible. 'Be in by eight, though. There's school tomorrow.'

'But Mum!' Her daughter seemed perversely reluctant, now, drat her! 'Who *is* that man?'

Amber watched Luke get out of the car. He was wearing denims now, but beautifully cut ones which showed exactly how well his body had withstood the ravages of ten years' hard living, and a casual shirt of softest brushed cotton. He brushed back the hair from his forehead with a swift, restless sweep of the hand, and her throat tightened inexplicably. She had seen that impatient gesture too many times in her dreams, the part of her memory she'd been unable completely to suppress.

'Oh, it's just someone from the university,' she said lightly. 'I expect it's something about work, darling.'

Kate hesitated a moment longer, then shrugged. Work was something boring her mother did every day, and cars, however fancy, were no substitute for horses.

'OK. I'm going to take Beauty for a spin,' she said. 'Lucy says to give her something else to think about!'

She passed Luke half-way up the path.

'Hi. Mum's inside,' Amber heard her call out breezily, before vaulting the fence, twitching her riding crop impatiently.

Amber opened the door before he had a chance to knock. There was little point in pretending she didn't know he was there—he must have seen her at the window.

'What do you want?' she asked bluntly.

He pretended to cringe.

'It's hardly the welcome Penelope gave Ulysses, is it?' he complained mildly. 'A few words will do, but is it possible for me to be allowed over the threshold?'

She shrugged and stood back, irrationally relieved that the dishes had been done, and the kitchen was at least clean.

'That, I assume, was Kate?' he said as he strolled casually into the kitchen. 'She's tall for her age, isn't she?'

'I suppose she is,' Amber conceded warily. 'She takes after me—I was always tall.'

'And her father, too?'

'Lawrence was over six foot,' Amber said. 'Would you like coffee? I was just about to have some. Or...something stronger?' She thought—hoped, having said it—that there was the remains of a bottle of whisky from last Christmas in the cupboard.

'Coffee will be fine,' he said. 'Were you horsey, too, at her age?'

'Goodness, no,' Amber said shortly, pouring water on to instant powder and hoping he wasn't expecting filtered coffee. 'I was a dreamy, intellectual child, with my head forever in a book.'

'And now you're a very practical secretary and mother,' he said. 'Strange, isn't it?'

There was always a question lurking behind his most casual comment, Amber thought. Always probing, digging, seeking out things one didn't want to be sought.

'I'm a single parent. It necessitates a different perspective. Milk and sugar?'

'Both, please,' he confirmed. 'So it's all been forgotten, has it—the books, the desire to write?'

'No, it hasn't——' she began exasperatedly, and then saw this ploy for what it was, a technique to make his subject reveal in anger what he or she might not otherwise. Although why he should care, she could not imagine. 'Would you like to come into the lounge?'

She prayed it would be at least tidy, as she couldn't remember what state they had left it in. Since they didn't have a dining-room, they mostly used the kitchen, and the lounge was only occupied in the evenings. It was a pleasant room, even if the carpet was a little shabby, furnished mostly with Amber's junk-shop finds, mellowed by the evening sun now streaming through the diamond-paned windows.

'I see the books are still part of your life,' he said, inspecting the alcoves either side of the chimney breast, full from wall to ceiling.

'Some of those were my husband's—he was a history lecturer—but yes, I still like to read,' Amber admitted. She shifted a pile of *Country Life* and *Horse and Pony* from a chair to the coffee-table. 'This is the limit of my daughter's literary interests, I'm afraid.'

She did not add that they were back numbers, passed on from Lucy, since magazines came expensive. Her financial status was none of his business. She wondered precisely what his business was, since he hadn't stated it, and the uncertainty was beginning to make her feel nervous. Glancing towards the ready-made pile of sticks and coals in the fireplace, she debated putting a match to it. The day had been warm, but the spring evenings still felt chilly. She decided against it. A fire would make the room more welcoming, and she didn't want him staying too long. He was used to warm climates. If he were cold, he'd soon leave.

But he took a seat, stretching out his legs comfortably and sipping his coffee as if it were finest Arabica, not supermarket granules. The thin, rangy tabby cat who had strayed into their home as a kitten and simply stayed, walked into the room with his tail in the air and stared pointedly at the visitor, ears pricked in an attitude both puzzled and irritated.

'Even the cat gives you a great reception here,' he said, unperturbed. 'Do you train him to repel intruders?'

'You're in his seat,' Amber said, with mean satisfaction.

Luke stretched out a hand—square, practical, with short, neat nails and surprisingly sensitive fingers—and tickled the cat behind its ear. And to Amber's disgust the traitorous, sycophantic creature began to purr and rub itself against him.

He laughed, as if sensing her annoyance.

'Cats are great sensualists,' he observed. 'This one is obviously used to a good deal of affection. I hope you don't lavish your entire attention on him, Amber.'

She stiffened. He was overstepping the boundaries of convention too easily. Just because once—*once*—they had made love, it did not give him the right to presume on that very old, very brief relationship, to make familiar remarks she found offensive.

'My attentions, and what I do with them, are no concern of yours,' she told him curtly.

He wasn't in the least abashed by her rebuff.

'No, they aren't,' he agreed. 'But you are so very touchy about something so unimportant, it's difficult to resist teasing you a little.'

Unimportant? It might have been unimportant to him—he had made that abundantly clear at the time. Amber sprang to her feet, trying hard to control the fit of inner trembling that had seized her.

'I think you had better go!' she said coldly.

And now the quick, sensitive hand was on her arm, actually touching her. A touch she had not known for years, but it, too, was as instantly recognisable as if it had caressed her only the day before.

'Please,' he said quietly, 'I promise to behave, and state my purpose. Sit down.

She did so, if only to put herself out of reach of his hand, and inside she was still cold and shaking, in the grip of a strange palsy she did not understand.

He said, 'I was told you solved departmental problems. I have a problem. I need somewhere congenial to live for the next three months.'

She gave a short laugh of amazement.

'Why ask me? The bursar's department deals with all that,' she told him.

'I know. They have—at least, they've given me a room in one of the halls of residence, which is fine for a few nights. But that won't do for a whole term. I want somewhere pleasant, comfortable, with a bit of style. Expense isn't a problem. Can you find me something by the end of the week?'

'It won't be easy. Accommodation is very tight around here.'

'But you're a miracle worker.' His voice was soft, almost purring with disbelief. 'Or so I've been told.'

It was a challenge she could not pass by.

'Leave it with me,' she said. 'I'll see what I can do.' And then, 'You know, you could have seen me about this tomorrow morning.'

'I could. But I have to acquaint myself with my new students at nine a.m., and by the time I'd be free, a whole morning would have been wasted. I don't work that way.'

And I, she itched to retort, don't expect people to come to my home unless they are my guests, whom I've invited. But her address was easy enough to find, so she could only hope he had got her message, and wouldn't take it on himself to call again.

He stood up in a leisurely, unconcerned manner which did not suggest her lack of enthusiasm for his visit had discomfited him.

'I'll be off now,' he said. 'I like your house, Amber, and your daughter. Even your cat. Thank you for the coffee, and the promise of assistance. One never knows how one will be received when one drops by unexpectedly.'

At first the allusion did not get through to her, but when it did her face began to burn. She saw herself, not quite eighteen, pushing her bicycle up the dusty drive towards the ramshackle Perigordian farmhouse he was renting, seeking out a man she had met only the day before, who had been kind enough to help her out of a dilemma. He had not asked her to go there; in fact, he had made it fairly clear he did not think it would be a good idea for them to meet again. But she was intrigued by him to the point of obsession, especially when, seeking directions to the farmhouse which he had told her only was near a village called Tarsac, she had learned, quite by accident, that the man who had introduced himself to her only as 'Luke' was in reality the foreign correspondent, Lucas Tremayne. The fame and fortune of his best-selling novel and film were still in the future, but his daring and irreverent dispatches from wartorn areas were already making him a name, and Amber was an early aficionado of his work.

She'd tracked him down, that was the truth of it. And when she'd seen the place where he was staying, abandoned, dilapidated, surrounded by great oaks and chestnut trees in full, whispering leaf, and deep in an overgrown wilderness of a garden, it was obvious he had gone there to lose himself. It was a retreat, and she had invaded it.

She hadn't deceived herself that he was ecstatic to see her, but it had been hot, she'd biked quite a way, and he hadn't turned her out. Instead, he'd poured her a glass of wine, and shared a crusty baguette with her.

'"A jug of wine, a loaf of bread—and thou beside me, singing in the wilderness,"' she recalled him saying flippantly. 'What more could we desire?'

He'd seemed deeply depressed when she'd arrived, and she had not known how to take this sudden, amused facetiousness. His fiercely alternating and unpredictable swings of mood had been confusing and incomprehensible to her, but they were part of what made him fascinating. Later, he had taken her properly out to lunch, and by that time she had been sure she was deeply in love with him.

Staring at him now, all these years on, hearing the gently implied rebuke in his voice, Amber swallowed hard and told herself *she* had no reason to feel guilty. He had been kind enough to her to begin with, but the way he had used her and finally dismissed her had been anything but kind.

But she had no wish to refer to that now. To do so would drag her into deeper waters, and she preferred to remain in the shallows. It was all history, anyhow, and could not be altered, so why disturb it?

She showed him to the door in silence, but in spite of her promise to herself the sight of the Jaguar triggered off her memory again.

'I take it this one is yours?' she said, with a touch of acid.

'Oh, yes.' He smiled slowly, and all at once she hated him, standing there in the radiant confidence of his glamour and riches and his fulfilled ambitions. 'I've passed the stage now where I need to borrow my agent's car.'

Head tilted slightly to one side, regarding her, he said, 'You remember far more, really, than you would have me believe, don't you, Amber?'

Of course she remembered! Unworldly teenage girls did not lose their virginity to their literary heroes every day of their lives! They were not seduced and dumped as an everyday occurrence!

'Not with any great pleasure, I can assure you,' she said coolly. 'Goodnight, Luke. I'll do what I can about finding you somewhere to live. And if you need to see me about that, or anything else, I'll be in my office.'

He raised a hand to his forehead in a brief, derisive salute.

'Yes, ma'am,' he said, in a tone of deep but entirely feigned respect.

She woke up in the small hours of the night, when it was still dark, from a dream that was startling in its sense of reality, so clear that she expected to find herself in the bedroom of the hotel at La Roque Gageac.

She was spending the summer in France with Uncle Selwyn, her guardian, a motoring tour which was a reward for all the hard work she had done for her A-levels. They had pottered gently down the Loire valley and on into the Limousin, Amber finding it all enchanting: the long, almost empty roads, the little towns with their country markets, the traditional *logis* where they stayed. On the third day, they crossed into the Perigord and checked in at an hotel in the little village clinging to a hillside, facing the broad, majestic sweep of the Dordogne river.

Then a sudden crisis had demanded Uncle Selwyn's return to England for a few days, leaving Amber alone in France, and for all that she was fond of her guardian, an elderly bachelor who had taken responsibility for her when her parents had died, she took a guilty delight in her unexpected freedom. She hired a bicycle—a pleasure she couldn't expect Uncle Selwyn to share—and rode along the riverbank, stopping to eat crusty bread and aromatic cheese, and to swim from tiny shingle beaches. Becoming more ambitious, she had set out to explore the ancient hilltop *bastide* of Domme, one of those fortified towns the English and French had built several centuries earlier, when they were fighting each other across the region.

The road from Cenac, in the valley, wound hairpin-like uphill, the sun was at its zenith, and Amber was hot, dusty and tired. Worse still, her bicycle had developed a puncture, and she had no puncture kit with her. She wheeled her unrideable machine in through the massive Porte des Tours, one of the gates admitting travellers through the ramparts around the town, and stood breathless and dejected in the beautiful main square, surrounded by medieval houses of glowing golden sandstone, with window-boxes and hanging baskets dripping pelargoniums and starry lobelia.

'*Hélas, mademoiselle,*' said an amused voice just behind her, '*ce n'était pas très malin, n'est-ce pas?*' That wasn't too bright of you, was it?

Amber sat straight up in bed in the cottage near Westbury, flushed and trembling. She could almost feel his breath on her bare shoulders, almost believe that she would turn round and look straight into the keenest, most analytical blue eyes she had ever seen, summing up her unfortunate situation at a glance.

Slowly, she relaxed, sinking back down on to her pillow. She was at home, it was the middle of the night, and the encounter she had dreamed about had taken place many years ago. All the same, even now, fully awake, she could not help reliving it.

Realising that she was a compatriot in distress, he had taken pity on her. The town was built high on a hill, sentinel over the surrounding countryside, and at its edge a beautiful bluff hung like a great balcony overlooking the broad valley of the Dordogne. Here they sat at a terrace table, Amber gratefully gulping down freshly squeezed lemon juice with water, while he drank a glass of pale golden beer.

They talked lightly. She told him about the motoring holiday, and how she was waiting for her uncle to return before they could continue on towards the Riviera. He told her a little about the place he was renting, near a small village not far from Les Eyzies.

'So far off the beaten track as to be out of sight. No tourist attractions. One shop, one restaurant— rather good—a few houses. Unimaginable peace.' He said the last words hungrily, like a starving man describing a banquet.

Amber was at a loss, thrown by this light and shade quality in him that hinted at unexpressed depths of sorrow and unplumbed fathoms of human experience she could only guess at. Who was he? What had he done, where had he been? He told her almost nothing, but offered to put the bike in the boot of his car and run her back to her hotel.

The car was a Jaguar, and made short work of the journey back to La Roque Gageac. Too short for

Amber, who was deeply intrigued by this fascinating stranger. She felt that this meeting had to be more than the random working of chance, that he had something to say to her, and to her alone. But he dropped her at the hotel and bid her a swift goodbye.

'Will I see you again?' she asked hesitantly.

'I think that would be most inadvisable,' he replied. 'Goodbye, Amber. Enjoy the rest of your holiday—and the rest of your life.'

It was a strange, unorthodox thing to say, but even then, in her youth and inexperience, she had known him at once for a strange, unorthodox man.

Amber tossed restlessly, unable to get back to sleep. In everyone's life there were innumerable 'maybe's and 'what if's, some trivial, some major turning points. She knew that day was one of the latter, for it was impossible to imagine how different the course of her life would have been if she had simply left her meeting with Luke as a chance encounter, instead of turning it into an adventure.

She stared into the darkness, trying to plot the course of that shadowy other life she might have lived, trying to see that very different woman she would have become. Not regretful, no, not that at all, but curious, as she recognised that on such small things as a burst tyre a destiny turns.

And in the truthful stillness of this quiet hour, she thought that, in a strange way, she should thank him for what she had gained, as much as blame him for what had been lost. Right now, she felt no rancour, no resentment, and no anger towards him, for all that he was rich and famous, and she was a hard-up nonentity, struggling to keep her ship afloat.

In the small bedroom next to hers, Amber heard Kate turn over, moaning softly in her sleep. She smiled and snuggled down again under her quilt, feeling indescribably smug and triumphant, full of a secret knowledge which was hers alone, and which she had no intention of imparting.

'Nuts to you, Lucas Tremayne!' she whispered cheerily into her pillow, settling down for what remained of the night. 'I can take anything *you* can throw at me, and come up smelling of roses!'

Of course, in the morning, she would not feel half so sanguine!

# CHAPTER THREE

THEY talked only in monosyllables and sawn-off phrases most mornings. Amber was usually busy trying to prepare breakfast, fix her daughter's packed lunch, and get herself ready for work all at the same time, while Kate was a disorganised heap of school books, PE kit and odd socks, wandering around with a piece of toast in one hand, and a three-day-old printed letter from school in the other.

So when her daughter asked 'What did he want?' Amber was able to translate the verbal shorthand at once.

'He wanted me to find him somewhere to live,' she replied. 'He's a temporary member of the department, and he wants something a little posher than the halls of residence.'

Kate peered into her sandwich box.

'Yuk, Mum, not cheese *again*! Is he rich?'

'Stinking,' Amber replied cheerfully. 'Ready now, Kate? Get into the car.'

Kate scrambled into the back of the Mini while Amber locked the cottage door. The next question came as she switched the engine into life.

'They aren't usually rich. Why's he different?'

Kate, an academic's daughter, had absorbed with her puréed carrots and toast soldiers the fact that academic salaries were not the stuff tax exiles were made of, Amber thought with a wry grin, wishing her daughter would not show such exceptional interest in this particular visitor.

'No, they aren't, darling, but this one's a writer who had a film made from one of his books, and it made him a lot of money.'

Kate digested this information without too much excitement. All her life she had been surrounded by people who wrote things. Students wrote theses, and graduates wrote post-doctoral treatises; her father had written various papers, and all the other lecturers and professors were always at it, too. Even her mother had sheaves of untidy manuscript she slaved over in odd bursts, then pushed back in the drawer. It was no big deal. Only the idea that someone actually made money out of it was different. But she wasn't overly impressed, and Amber was proud of the well-adjusted attitude of this child who had grown up with making-do and second-hand. She wouldn't be fretting to meet Lucas Tremayne on account of his wealth and celebrity status.

Breathing more easily, she pulled up by the school gates.

'Here you are, love. See you tonight.'

She spent most of that morning phoning round estate agents, ferreting out likely properties to rent. Foolishly, she realised, she had not asked Luke for any precise requirements. Something pleasant, comfortable, with a bit of style, was all he had said. Expense no problem, of course. But did he want to live actually in Westbury, or in the country? A flat or a house? Was a garden essential, was proximity to the university a crucial factor? He was on his own, but would he want to entertain, have people to stay? Would guest bedrooms be required?

Really, she ought to refer back to him for more detailed information, but she was reluctant to do so. He had issued her a challenge, and she wanted to find him a triumph of a home, out of a hat.

'But you're a miracle worker,' he had said tauntingly. She wanted to spite him by coming up with an appropriate miracle.

But it was not going to be that simple, she thought, as she phoned her sixth estate agent. Property to let was in short supply in a small town with a heavy influx of academic families.

'Of course,' the girl at the estate agent's said diffidently, 'there's always the old Arkwright place. The present owner's gone abroad for a year, and we're instructed to let it, but it's a very individual house . . . and its macabre history puts a lot of people off.'

A gleam of pure mischief shone in Amber's green eyes. She knew the place. Out on the very edge of Westbury, in what had been deepest countryside when it was built by an early industrialist, the house was right by the river, on the site of an old mill, with the wheel still *in situ*. Nothing good ever happened to Arkwright *père* from the moment he moved his family in. A daughter had gone mad, two sons had been killed in foreign wars, the business had failed, and the old man and his wife had died in questionable circumstances—it was said he had killed her and himself. Some rumoured that the place was haunted, as well it might be.

'This is a very individual tenant, and I doubt he'd be deterred by the odd ghost,' Amber said, sticking it on her list. She decided to devote her lunch break to checking it out. If it turned out to have a leaking roof and rising damp, she'd have egg all over her face.

But Luke surprised her by walking into the office just as she was about to set off.

If a lecture-room full of enquiring undergraduates had worried him at all, he showed no sign of it. His smile displayed the same blend of humour and cynicism it always did.

'How was the lecture?' she could not resist asking curiously.

'Oh, I'll survive, if the students will,' he replied laconically. 'What's more to the point, how's the house-hunting?'

She shrugged. 'As I told you, there isn't much available, but I've managed to find a few possibilities. Two flats, fairly central, a three-bed semi in a suburb a little further out, and a . . . a house by the river.'

'The two flats and the semi don't sound much to write home about,' he said, as she had fully expected he might. 'The house by the river might be interesting.'

'I've collected the keys, and I was about to check it out,' Amber said. 'It hasn't been lived in for some time, and I'm not sure what state it's in.'

He glanced at his watch.

'In your lunch hour? Such devotion to duty,' he said. 'I'll come with you.'

That she had not expected. Not only would she feel a fool, her mischievous impulse backfiring on her if the place turned out to be uninhabitable, but she would be forced into his company for the best part of an hour, and her intention was to see less of Lucas Tremayne, not more.

'It might be a mess,' she demurred, 'then you'll have wasted your time.'

'So what? It's my time, and I want to see the house. After all, I'm the one who might be renting it,' he said, reasonably enough. 'Come on—we'll take my car. I'm not so sure yours isn't held together with bits of string.'

That too was unexpected and undesirable. The person who drove was somehow in control, and she did not want to permit him to control any part of her life, even an hour of her time.

'There's nothing wrong with my car,' she said indignantly, sliding into the passenger seat of the sleek, feline Jaguar.

'If you say so,' he agreed, laughing. 'But mine will get us there more quickly.'

'Not if every traffic light in Westbury is against us,' she muttered argumentatively.

He shot her a glance that was both amused and exasperated.

'Belt up and shut up,' he ordered. 'You've become very stroppy in your old age, Amber Sinclair.'

'Mrs Kingsland, to you,' she reminded him. 'And you've become dictatorial in yours.'

He laughed again, and she thought how unfair it was that he was so amusedly unconcerned by her reappearance in his life, while she was thrown into such deep mental turbulence by his. Every light was obligingly green as they sped smoothly through town, as if to demonstrate to her that things went his way, and would always go his way. In no time at all they had reached the outskirts of the town, and there was the house, on its own, with trees all around it, and the rushing sound of the water which had once turned the mill filling their ears.

They got out of the car, and Luke stood quietly for a while, hands thrust deep into the pockets of his suede jacket.

'Why did you think this house would appeal to me, Amber?' he said at length, and all the amusement had left his voice now—and his eyes, too. He was deadly serious in his questioning, and his sudden sobriety caught her off balance.

'I . . . I don't know,' she answered unsteadily.

'I think you do,' he said, regarding her with unwelcome directness. 'It reminded you of the farmhouse at Tarsac, didn't it? You figured I would want a rural retreat, a hideaway.'

'No,' she denied hotly. 'That's not what I thought. Why should it even have entered my head?'

But had it—subconsciously, at least? He was still looking at her with that deathly quiet intentness which made her want to look away, but she didn't dare. She was held captive.

'Because you're hung up on the idea of the man I was then,' he said. 'Put it out of your mind, Amber. I'm not that man. Any more than you are that girl.'

She could think of nothing sensible to say. He had teased her mildly, on and off, with the occasional slightly salacious reference to their past association. But now, if she understood him correctly, he was telling her that he had changed. The man who had once briefly found her desirable no longer existed, and he wasn't in the least attracted to her.

She should have been immensely relieved to hear it. If he didn't find her attractive, he would not pursue her, and, the less contact they had, the easier the past would lie buried—as she wanted it to.

All the same, she felt she was being rejected all over again, and it would have been difficult for her, as a woman, not to be a little piqued by that. But should she feel quite such a deep sense of hurt?

'Perhaps we had better go and look at the flats?' she suggested quietly.

'No,' he said, with unexpected emphasis. 'Since we're here, we might as well look.'

Inside, Amber was comforted to see, the house was clean and dry. The carpets were good, the curtains had recently been dry-cleaned, and the faint chill was nothing a good fire wouldn't banish. She hadn't brought him to see a broken-down ruin.

'Adam fireplaces,' Luke noted approvingly. 'Some of the furniture is Georgian, too. In fact, it's quite an impressive house. Strange that no one lives permanently in it.'

'It has a history,' Amber murmured. 'The original owner's family all came to grief. Locally, it's known as Arkwright's Folly.'

Amused eyebrows rose over the keen blue eyes.

'Why, Amber—you don't meant to tell me that you've brought me to see a haunted house? You little devil, you! How d'you know I don't have a supremely nervous temperament?'

Amber shivered. He was jocular and unconcerned, but something about the sound of the water rushing past the windows of the lounge where they stood unnerved her, filling her with an awareness of ancient sorrows.

'Can we go, please?' she asked, trying to sound casual. 'Surely you've seen enough?'

'Plenty,' he agreed cheerfully. 'I'll take it. And I withdraw my doubts. You *are* a clever girl—every bit as clever as the professor says.'

She couldn't stifle a gasp.

'You mean you intend to live here? You can't be serious?' she exclaimed.

'Can't I?' He tossed the question lightly back at her. 'Then why did you bring me to look at the place, if you didn't think I'd be interested?'

He glanced around briefly, strode over to the window and gazed out at the fast running river.

'Why not? I'll invite a few friends down, have a house party. It should prove quite a talking point. Who knows—perhaps I'll get lucky, and one of the resident ghosts will oblige.'

Amber turned away, a faint exhalation of annoyance escaping her. She had put this house on her list as a kind of black joke, but he had called her bluff, and now the joke was on her. He would make a big thing of telling everyone how smart she had been to find it for him, and all the time she would know that he had seen through her ruse, and was sending her up.

And beneath the banter would be yet another, deeper message, for her alone. Don't think, he would be telling her, that this is another Tarsac. Don't think that I have any intention of spiriting you away here and making love to you. You might have had your charm when you were seventeen and I was at a loose end, but those days are long gone, and you couldn't hold my interest now.

Another tremor shook her and, noting it, he left the window and came quickly to her side. His hand rested lightly on her shoulder, and through the material of her thin summer jacket and the blouse beneath she swore she could feel its touch burning her flesh. Moving it very slightly, he fingered the lapel of her blouse, rubbing it between thumb and forefinger, and she felt that imprint, too, on the skin beneath it.

It had not changed. Whatever else she might feel about this man—anger, resentment, fear of the upset he could cause in her careful little world—the physical response of her body to the touch of his hand was as disturbing and instantaneous now as it had been when she was seventeen, and could betray her as easily.

'There's nothing to worry about,' he said softly. 'I'm not afraid of ghosts any more.'

'Perhaps I am,' Amber said ambiguously. 'Let's go now, Luke.'

She was glad to get away from the house and the river, and did not look back as he started the car and began to drive. He was wrong—it wasn't at all like the old farmhouse at Tarsac. That had been run-down and sunk in rural somnolence, but it had radiated peace, whereas this one evoked only gloom.

But, if he really insisted on living here, that was nothing to do with her. She supposed she wouldn't be invited again, either singly or to his silly house party. And I wouldn't come if I were, she thought with a shudder, recalling another occasion when she had dropped in on Luke and his literary friends. She'd felt foolish and unnecessary then, and didn't imagine it would be any different, now.

Luke did not drive directly back to the university, but instead turned into the car park of a pub not far from the house.

'Having settled that satisfactorily, I think we're entitled to break for lunch,' he said.

Amber cast him a startled glance. Lunch—together?

'No, really, I should be getting back to work,' she protested. 'Professor Doyle——'

'Has gone to the standing committee, and anyhow, taking care of members of staff is part of your job,' he interrupted smoothly.

'But I finish at three-thirty—my afternoon will be half over by the time I get back,' she said.

'Oh, come on, Amber,' he said testily. 'At least let's have a drink and a sandwich to sustain us. I'm not suggesting we indulge in a bacchanalian orgy of eating.'

If they had been in her car, none of this would have happened, she reflected, remembering her initial misgivings. But they weren't, and she could either accompany him inside, or sit and sulk in the car park. She followed him into the lounge, mouth set firmly with disapproval.

'I trust you've progressed from *citron pressé*,' he said, as they threaded their way to a vacant table.

'White wine—dry, please,' Amber said, reminding herself that she had both to work and to drive herself home, later.

They ate roast beef on crusty bread, garnished with salad—the simplest of food, but he seemed to relish it.

'The English pub is one of the things you miss when you spend a lot of time abroad,' he said. 'Along with fish and chips out of paper bags, and milk bottles clanking on the step in the mornings. Have you done much travelling, Amber?'

'I haven't had the——' She was going to say "money" but very quickly substituted "opportunity". She and Lawrence had been pushed financially at first, to buy the cottage on a junior research fellow's grant. The lectureship had just begun to make things a little easier when he'd died, leaving her, by an unfortunate oversight, unprovided for. Since then, such luxuries had been out of the question. She paid her mortgage, kept Kate and herself—just—and that was it.

'I haven't been abroad since I went to France with Uncle Selwyn,' she said shortly.

His gaze was both enquiring and perceptive.

'No? Well, it was your choice to marry young and start a family early, I suppose,' he said.

'That's right,' Amber agreed, tight-lipped. 'It was. I'm not complaining, just stating a fact.'

'Naturally.' Why did she have the feeling that he did not believe her? 'And how is your uncle, these days?'

'Uncle Selwyn died two years ago,' Amber said, draining her wine with more haste than she had intended.

'Amber, I'm sorry.' He sounded as if he genuinely was, she thought, surprised. 'Your life seems to have had more than its fair share of sorrows over the past few years. Here——' he noted her empty glass '—let me get you a refill for that.'

'No—thank you.' She put a hand over the top of it, shaking her head. 'I'd rather not, truly. Living where we do, I can't afford to risk losing my driving licence. There are very few buses, and I have to get to work.'

'Do you really—have to, I mean?' He was probing again, digging deeper into herself and her motives than she was prepared for him to delve. 'Wouldn't it be preferable to stay at home while your daughter is so young? She needs you as a basis for her life.'

'She *has* me. Just because I work doesn't mean I don't care. I do, and Kate knows it,' Amber retorted with controlled anger. 'I'm home not long after she finishes school, and the holidays fit in with hers. Don't be so old-fashioned, Luke. Lots of women with children Kate's age, and even younger, have jobs. I suppose if *you* had a family, you'd think it perfectly OK to go swanning off around the globe, but your wife would have to be tied to the hearth!'

Her indignation was genuine, but she was glad to give full vent to it, as it provided a smoke-screen for her real reason for working—absolute financial necessity. She preferred him to think she was one of those women who went out to work for the fun of it.

'"Swanning round the globe" happens to be what I'm paid to do,' he pointed out. 'It's hypothetical, of course, since I'm not married, but if I had a family, my wife would need to be the stay-put kind.'

And now Amber could not resist a little delicate probing of her own, very cautious and tentative.

'But you were married, once, weren't you—to a photographer? I would have thought that was a fairly mobile profession.'

'That was different,' he said shortly. 'Gemma would never have wanted children. We planned an open marriage—seeing each other when our schedules fitted, not tying each other down too much.'

'Then why——' She bit her lip, clamped her mouth shut. Probing might be second nature to him, but she was shy of invading anyone else's space too importunately.

'Why marry at all?' He finished the question for her. 'People marry for all kinds of reasons, Amber. Romantic delusion, impulse, security, convenience ... you name it. None of them is a guarantee of success.'

He downed the rest of his drink swiftly.

'I'm not in a position to say whether mine would have worked or not. You had a little longer. Did you find the magic elixir?'

Amber stared at him, affronted not so much by his curiosity but by her own inability to satisfy it as she would have wished. She would dearly have loved to say, Yes, I did. Those few years Lawrence and I had together were perfect. But it wasn't strictly true. They had been troubled by his jealousy and her guilt, and who knew if, given time, they would have been able to resolve that?

'I don't want to discuss my marriage with you,' she said coldly.

He shrugged.

'OK. I overstepped the mark. A thick skin is another journalistic accoutrement, so I'm accustomed to the occasional put-down,' he said easily. And then he added something which to Amber's ears had an ominous ring. 'Sometimes, what people refuse to tell you is as informative as what they do say.'

It was a quiet afternoon in the Department of English. Everyone was out or occupied, and Amber was able to get on with simple, repetitive jobs like the filing, which had been steadily mounting up. But the trouble with simple, repetitive jobs was that they only kept the hands and the surface layer of one's mind busy, freeing the higher faculties of memory and emotion and giving them ample scope to wander.

Hers wandered back to a verdant valley where a small, natural lake filled a declivity in the ground, well-screened by trees and invisible to anyone not aware of its presence. A little stream fed into it at one end and disappeared via some subterranean exit, wild flowers grew along the banks, and dragonflies darted and hovered, their gossamer wings reflecting the sunlight.

Here, Amber and Luke swam after their memorable lunch at the Auberge du Pont in Tarsac. The water, as he had warned her, came from high up in the hills, and was icy cold, even on the hottest of days; she remembered the delicious, freezing chill of it on her skin as she plunged in.

Remembered, too, the fascination of watching his body as he swam: the long, clean furrow of his back, the strong, forceful arms, the ripple of pectorals as he turned over into a leisurely backstroke. She could not take her eyes from him, and was embarrassed by her preoccupation with his physical presence.

Afterwards he spread towels on the grass beneath the trees, and they lay letting the sun dry them naturally. They were not touching, but she could feel his body-warmth; not speaking, but she could hear the slow intake and exhalation of his breath. For the moment, his restlessness seemed to be calmed, and she was utterly content, thinking he was equally happy to be with her.

His eyes were closed, and she realised he had drifted off to sleep. As she shook out her damp hair, little droplets of water fell on to his chest, and she smoothed them lightly with her fingertips, not disturbing him, but relishing how good his skin felt to her touch. She observed him minutely, as if she wanted to imprint the fine details on the receptive screen of her mind forever: the haphazard crescent of freckles across his nose, the assertive jaw, the wryly humorous, cynical curve of his mouth.

'I love you,' she whispered almost under her breath, full of wonder at how swiftly and unexpectedly it had happened to her, just as all the poets and song-writers promised it did.

Suddenly, he had stirred restlessly, moving his head from side to side, clenching his hands tightly. He sat bolt upright, staring at her but not seeing her, gazing into some horror visible only to himself.

'Gemma!' he cried hoarsely. 'For heaven's sake— the whole house is going to go! *Move!* Give me your hand—forget the bloody cameras! Gemma! Where the hell are you? I can't see you!'

His jaw worked, sweat broke out on his forehead, and yet he was shivering violently. Amber felt shut out, excluded by this very personal nightmare which was gripping him; she put her hands on his shoulders and shook him gently.

'Luke—Luke—it was only a dream,' she said. 'It's me—Amber. We're here, at Tarsac.'

His eyes focused on her then.

'Amber?' he said distantly. She brushed his face with the fingertips of one hand, wanting to restore the sunlit contentment and the sense of togetherness which had somehow been lost. Her touch seemed to wake something in him, and turning his head to one side he kissed the palm that had caressed his cheek.

'Oh, you're so sweet, so lovely, so utterly re-freshing,' he murmured into it. 'Just to look at you makes me feel new again. You don't know how much I want to kiss you!'

She made a little, incoherent sound of assent, and it was impossible to say which of them made the first move. She was in his arms, his face buried in the still damp, fragrant mass of her hair, and she was full of relief and gladness that he was hers again, the bad moments banished.

Tremulously but willingly, she lifted her mouth to his, waiting for the romantic consummation of his kiss to tell her he loved her, too. But the moment his lips touched hers, they were doomed. She was on fire with a warm, singing sensation, and her very eagerness ignited him with its intensity. He kissed her repeatedly; his hands, planted on her hips just above the line of her bikini, caressed her skin softly, gliding over the hipbone and upwards to her waist.

Amber was weeks short of her eighteenth birthday, she'd had a sheltered upbringing with her elderly guardian, and no one had ever before touched her so intimately. But this was Luke, she loved him, and surely he must feel the same about her? It couldn't be wrong. A small cry of alarm escaped her as he released the catch of her bikini top, but she did not seriously protest, and modesty was swiftly overcome by pleasure as his questing hands and then his mouth discovered her breasts.

There was nothing on earth then that could have prevented the fulfilment of this fiercely aroused desire. She was awed and amazed that a man could be so beautiful, that he could be so gentle and yet so strong inside her, each deep, thrusting movement bringing her a new definition of pleasure. She matched him joyously, striving towards the final, flooding moment of ecstasy, hardly aware of feeling any pain at all. Afterwards, a deep, indescribable peacefulness enveloped her. She had not known that one human being could bring such serene completeness to another.

But Luke, she realised, was far from serene. Now that his breathing had returned to normal, his face was full of consternation—and regret.

'Luke? What's wrong?' An awful suspicion had seized her. 'Wasn't I very good? I've...I've never done that before.'

'Oh lord, Amber, don't rub it in!' he said in a low voice. 'I don't need telling that you were a virgin! I feel as guilty as hell—what could I have been thinking of?'

But we love each other, she wanted to say. I'm yours now, and you're mine. What is there to feel guilty about?

'Don't spoil it,' she begged in a small, puzzled whisper. 'It was wonderful. We can...we can do it again—if you like.'

He looked at her very strangely, but his voice when he spoke was decisive.

'I think not,' he said. 'Put your clothes on, Amber, and I'll take you home. Believe me, I didn't plan it this way.'

She had not talked much on the way back to the hotel. For one thing, she had been deeply pre-occupied in thinking over what had happened—the dizzy, terrifying, marvellous process of falling in love, which was in itself enough to turn her universe upside-down. And making love—the wonder of touching and being touched, the endlessly exciting sensations, sweeter than she had ever known existed.

But she was not too lost in analysis of her own emotions to be unaware of the brooding darkness of

Luke's manner, and she struggled to understand what was troubling him.

So she had been a virgin—but no one could stay a virgin forever! Sooner or later we all fall in love and give ourselves to someone, she mused, stealing an uncertain glance at his grim, hard profile. He shouldn't blame himself, since she had been far from unwilling—it wasn't as if he had ravished her against her protests.

Maybe it would have been better to lose her virginity on her wedding night, but Amber wondered how many girls waited that long these days. Love was the main thing. She loved him, trusted him, and desired only to be his from now onward. Nothing else mattered. He'd realise that, too, when he'd had time to think about it.

So she sat demurely by his side, saying nothing, asking no questions, making herself be content to wait his time, sure that it would come.

'I'll call you,' was all he said, briefly, as he dropped her at the hotel. 'Don't worry—it will be all right.'

And she believed him then, with all her heart, Amber remembered now, gazing out at the trees in the quadrangle, snowy with blossom. How naïve and foolish she had been, in her innocence, going up to her room with her head full of romantic dreams, longing eagerly for tomorrow to come, a tomorrow when she would fall into his arms, never to be parted from him again.

She could well imagine now what *he* had been thinking as he drove back to his solitary farmhouse.

Oh, hell, I must need my head inspecting! The wretched girl was a virgin—who'd have thought so, the way she was panting for it? And it was hardly worth the trouble! Let's hope she doesn't make a fuss, and I haven't gone and put her in the club!

Amber sniffed disgustedly, the May loveliness of the trees completely lost on her for once. For a moment, back there in the house by the river, she had felt once more that sensual tug of excitement, so strong that she almost forgot how he had once hurt her.

He must never know—she must be sure never to let him know—that he still had that power to stir her. Just as she would do all in *her* power to prevent him from learning that he was the father of a living child, conceived on a hot, still afternoon in the Perigord by a girl who had meant nothing to him.

# CHAPTER FOUR

THE LECTURES given by Luke Tremayne proved to be a great success with the students of Westbury's English Department—as she might have known all along that they would be, Amber thought disgustedly. Was there anything that man could not do successfully? Was it too much to nurse a secret, malicious hope that one day he might fall flat on his all too engaging face?

'For a start, his choice of material surprised everyone,' Cal said enthusiastically. 'It would have been natural for him to take as his poetry choice war poets—Sassoon, Brooke, you know? Or perhaps a hell-raiser like Dylan Thomas, with whom you'd expect him to identify. So what does he do? He chooses Gerard Manley Hopkins, an obscure, nineteenth-century Jesuit priest, unpublished in his lifetime, whose style was light years ahead of anything being written at that time.'

'Um,' Amber said non-committally, promising herself to dig a volume of Hopkins out of the library and acquaint herself with his work, just out of curiosity, of course.

'His lectures certainly are—well, different,' Sorrel drawled, raising a languid eyebrow in Cal's direction. 'You should sit in on one or two, Cal, as I did. You might pick up a few tips. For sure, no one's going to fall asleep in there!'

Cal bristled visibly.

'No one falls asleep during my lectures, baby—if they do, I sling chalk at them! But neither you nor I can intersperse ours with funny journalistic anecdotes, as he apparently does. Like the one about being unceremoniously deported from some banana republic on his very first foreign assignment, and reporting back to his editor in fear and trembling, only to be warmly welcomed and slapped on the back. He hadn't realised no foreign reporter is "blooded" until he has been slung out of somewhere for telling the unpalatable truth.'

Amber, jolted out of her pretence of not really listening to this conversation which was taking place in her office gave a disparaging sniff. She'd heard that one over the *tarte aux abricots*, years ago, at the Auberge du Pont. Probably he used stories of his exploits as a softening up for seduction exercise. And now they were enlivening his lectures, too.

'Some of the incidents are downright hair-raising,' Sorrel observed. 'There was one about when he was with that African guerrilla outfit, got separated from his unit in the thick of night, and was picked up by a patrol from his own side. But they, not recognising this strange white man, thought he was a spy, and he had to stand there for the best part of half an hour, listening to them debating whether to shoot him outright or try to verify his story. I mean—it's like something straight out of Joseph Conrad!'

In spite of her affected indifference, Amber could not repress a shudder. She knew these were not merely tall stories. Luke really had been in all those wild places, done those crazy, dangerous things.

'What sort of man deliberately exposes himself to that kind of peril?' she mused aloud, with incredulous distaste.

'One who wants to get at the truth, perhaps?' Cal suggested. 'You don't much care for him, do you, Amber?'

She shrugged. 'I don't have any feelings one way or the other. But I think he's probably playing at Robin Hood. It's one way of escaping settling down and making any commitment.'

'Writing books like *When the Guns are Silent* doesn't require any commitment, in your opinion?'

'Yes, it does, but——'

'Amber means on the personal level,' Sorrel interjected with a little smile. 'She thinks Luke should hang up his notebook and Press card and become a regular family man. But every man isn't like Lawrence, Amber.'

'Take it easy, smart ass!' Cal jumped at once to Amber's defence, but she shook her head and smiled.

'It's all right, Cal, I don't mind,' she assured him. 'Excuse me—I have to go down to the photocopying machine and get these senate reports run off.'

She escaped swiftly, but as she hurried along the corridor, she couldn't help feeling like a phoney. Of course, Lawrence had been dead for five years, and she could reasonably be expected to have recovered from the early rush of grief. And there had been a time when she had been unable to talk about him. It had lasted for quite a while, and when she came to work at the university everyone had been kind and solicitous, seeing her as the grieving young widow of their colleague.

But her anguish had been on account of her failure to give Lawrence what he needed from her—an unconditional love with no backward glances, the reassurance that the past meant nothing, and another child, this time one who was truly his. He had died without her being able to give him any of these things, and *that* was what had tied her emotions in knots for some time afterwards. She had only begun to live as she emerged from the shadow of that guilt.

He had known from the beginning that she was in love with the man who had fathered her child, and assured her that it did not matter, that he loved *her*, and would accept her as she was, hoping that in time love would grown between them.

And in a way it had. Certainly Amber had grown deeply fond of him, she had done her utmost to be a good wife, and was desperately disappointed when she failed to become pregnant again. She had suggested a specialist, but he had refused that, with male pride, feeling that it must be his fault, since Amber had conceived Kate all too easily. This lack hung heavy between them, as did his constant awareness that she had once loved someone else, passionately, even though she told him repeatedly that it was over, forgotten, a one-off experience that she had no desire to be reminded of. She knew he never quite believed her, particularly as she had always insisted on keeping the real identity of Kate's father to herself.

'If you persist in hiding the knowledge from me, you're going to have to hide it from her, too,' he had challenged her more than once. 'It's only fair, Amber. I love that kid. I've looked after her, cared for her—*been* her father. Are you going to turn round one day and tell her it's not so?'

'She's not much more than a baby, Lawrence,' Kate had protested, knowing that she was avoiding the issue. 'We don't even have to think about it for a long time yet.'

But she did think about it, often, if only in the privacy of her own heart. Lawrence was right in one respect. A father had to be more than a biological accident, quickly forgotten. Whatever differences he and she had, he did think the world of Kate, and she loved him too. Wasn't that enough? Did her daughter ever have to know that she was the child of a dynamic but unreliable individual who racketed around the world putting his own life in jeopardy, and leaving behind a trail of deserted women? Lawrence was solid and dependable—surely a better male role model for a growing girl?

Only . . . inside her, that stubborn voice kept on insisting, but it's not the *truth*. She had silenced it resolutely. There was truth . . . and there was truth. This truth would only hurt Kate, Amber was more convinced of it than ever now. Kate was secure in her memories of the man she had called 'Daddy', of her sure, unequivocal place as part of a real family. Lawrence's death had not changed that. Removing him from the place he still occupied in Kate's scheme of things, and substituting another man, any man, but especially someone like Luke Tremayne, damn it— that would be madness!

Everyone at Westbury, not knowing the true story, assumed that Lawrence and Amber's had been a youthful love-match, sadly cut off in its prime. She never did anything to alter that view. Lawrence had been good to her in her way, and for his sake as much as her own she kept the illusion of a happy, united young family enshrined as memory. She felt she owed him that much, owed him, too, a child who looked back on him with affection as her father.

For herself, it no longer hurt to think or speak of him. The years alone had made her her own woman, no longer striving to fill anyone else's ideal, or be what she could not. Sorrel's casually bitchy comment had not troubled her on account of Lawrence. The truth was, it was talking about *Luke* that caused her pain, transporting her back unwillingly to the time before she had been a wife and mother, when she had loved him.

In the few short weeks he had been at Westbury, she had done her best to avoid him without making it too obvious that was what she was doing. It was not an easy balance to strike, and consisted of careful timing—turning up late for lunchtime sessions in the pub, and leaving early, always with an impeccable excuse. Attending just as few of the university social occasions as she could get away with, without anyone's noting or remarking on her absences.

Not having a sitter was a good standby of a get-out for evening events, so long as she didn't overdo it. If anyone asked 'What about your friend, Lucy?' she could always plead Lucy's heavy involvement with her current boyfriend. Lucy, she thought grimly, would kill her if she ever got to hear from any source that she was supposed to have turned Amber down!

She always made sure that if she were obliged to be in the same place as Luke, she did not take a seat too close to him, or join for too long any group of which he was a member. This, too, had to be finely judged so it appeared casual and accidental, not contrived. She had to talk to him sometimes, if only so that her not talking to him did not cause raised eye-brows. Universities were hotbeds of gossip, where people watched and commented upon one another's behaviour minutely, and these were not easy-to-fool idiots, but aware, intelligent, sharp-witted individuals.

So far, she congratulated herself, it was working. No one had any inkling that she and Luke had met before, or were other than new and casual working acquaintances. And, she had to admit, he had kept his word and not given her away, assuming, she supposed, that what she was anxious to protect was her reputation as a virtuous young widow. He had dropped no hints, and there had been no sly, knowing glances to make her blush, no comments intended to trip her up.

In fact, apart from those first few days, when any reference to the past had been made privately, in her hearing only, it was as if he had indeed forgotten that she was the girl he had met and made love to in France. Which only went to prove, she told herself soberly, that it had indeed been no more than an insignificant episode in his eventful life, and after the first surprise of meeting her again had passed he had probably thought no more about it. There had been no more visits to the cottage, no more uncomfortable questions about Kate, or her own life.

I've ceased to exist for him, she thought. I'm just Amber, the girl in the office. That's what you wanted, she answered herself, a low profile, so be thankful, can't you? You don't want him to disrupt your existence, you certainly don't want him to learn the truth about Kate. So sit tight, let the term pass quickly, as it will, and let him go. It's unlikely he'll ever come back again.

But it had to be admitted that those few occasions when she'd stood in the full spotlight of his interrogative attention, fencing off his questions, when she had been close enough to be drawn by the physical magnetism he still possessed for her—in those moments, she had been alive as she had not been in years. Alive as a woman. It had been raw, painful and difficult, and also real, exciting and meaningful, which was the obverse side of the same coin.

'How many copies of that report do you want, Amber?'

It was one of the other secretaries, watching, amused, as she absently fed paper into the copier, lost in her own thoughts.

'Lord, not *that* many!' Amber switched off the machine with a grin.

'You must have been daydreaming,' the girl laughed. 'Hope he was worth it!'

'He?' Amber laughed, too. 'Nothing so romantic, I'm afraid. I was working out my shopping list.'

And thus one lie led automatically to another, since she couldn't stand about with a soppy look on her face and start a rumour on the gravpevine that the solitary Mrs Kingsland at last had a man in her life! Two and two would soon be put together and making five—there was that rakishly attractive Lucas Tremayne who had set all hearts a-flutter, actually working in her department; obviously, she fancied him, too. Once such an idea gained credence, Amber knew it would spread like wildfire, and there would be very little she could do to put it out.

She walked briskly back to her office, and there, perched on the edge of her desk, she found the said Luke Tremayne, doodling on her telephone pad. The mere fact of his being there, when he had been so recently on her mind, made her start guiltily. It was some time since they had been alone together—not, in fact, since she had taken him to see the river house, where now, true to his stated intention, he was living.

She set down the reports on her desk and, inadvertently glancing at the sketch he'd drawn on her pad, could not repress a chuckle; it was a witty, if rather cruel caricature of a well-known political figure.

'That's not bad at all,' she said. 'I didn't know you could draw as well. You could illustrate your own articles!'

'And put someone else out of a job?' He laughed. 'It's just a knack the *Examiner*'s cartoonist taught me, how to exaggerate the salient points of someone's face.'

He sketched a few quick lines and, catching her breath, Amber recognised her own face in the triangle with the mass of squiggly hair and two huge, elongated eyes.

'Is that supposed to be me? Very droll,' she said drily. 'A man of many parts, aren't you?'

'Some you haven't even imagined, Amber,' he agreed, grinning at her. She took a long, deep breath. It was happening again. Inside her, something uncurled and stretched, glowed, came to life, trembling with the possibility of conflict and stimulation. She had to tread firmly on this infant life-form before it grew to an unmanageable and demanding maturity. It was dangerous, and she could not afford to nurture it.

'Was there something you wanted?' she asked coolly.

He tossed a small envelope on to the desk.

'Only to deliver this. I could have left it on your desk, I suppose, but—I don't know, Amber, we seem to be no more than ships that pass in the night recently,' he said, quite casually, but something in his voice brought her up sharp against the realisation that *he* was aware of her manoeuvres, if no one else was.

'That's all we ever were, Luke,' she said lightly.

The smile was mildly reminiscent now.

'We did come alongside once,' he said. 'Now don't jump down my throat—I know I promised to be a good boy, and not refer to our... liaison. And I haven't—not in public, anyhow.' He nodded towards the envelope. 'This is an invitation to my house-warming. Saturday evening, so as it's only Monday, I've given you plenty of notice.'

'That's kind of you, Luke,' Amber said in a measured, even tone which took a lot of effort to produce. 'But I don't know if I'll be able to come.'

'You have a prior engagement? What a shame,' he drawled mockingly.

Adept as she had become at twisting facts, Amber found herself annoyingly unable to tell him this small, barefaced lie.

'No, I...' She faltered. 'Well, it's not easy. Sitters, and so forth, you know.'

'You *do* have five days to find one,' he pointed out. 'However, if you can't, you could always bring Kate along. It will be a very circumspect party—university people and a few of my friends from London who are eager to see my provincial seclusion. Seven-thirty, all right?'

'I'll... I'll see,' she replied a little ungraciously, wondering why he should be so insistent that she came. Was he intent on embarrassing her all over again?

Amber's determined little chin went up, her shoulders squared. It wouldn't be that easy now. She would not be a confused, love-lorn seventeen-year-old, alone among a group of sophisticates, but a woman on her own ground, surrounded by other people she knew and liked.

'Saturday, then?' he said. 'Although I expect I shall see you before.'

She decided she would be non-committal about her acceptance or refusal of the invitation until Friday afternoon, then at the last minute she would invent some cast-iron reason why, regretfully, she would be unable to come. He could believe her or not, but at that late stage in the proceedings there would be very little he, or anyone else, could do about it.

Her plot was sabotaged on Wednesday morning by Professor Doyle.

'Have you had your invitation to Mr Tremayne's party?' he asked in the middle of dictating some letters.

'Er—yes, actually,' Amber replied, startled by the query. He did not usually enquire into her after-work activities.

'Good. I hope to see you there,' he said, quietly but firmly. 'Mr Tremayne is something of a feather in the department's cap. His lectures are working out even better than I could have hoped, and he's giving us his time for a pittance, really, to him. I feel it's important for all departmental staff to show our appreciation by being present.'

'Even me?' she asked, in a tone of surprised self-deprecation, and the grey eyebrows rose above the horn-rimmed spectacles.

'You are a member of the department, are you not? And a very valued and important one,' he said. 'There are occasions when we have to demonstrate the meaning of that word which is so fashionable now-adays—solidarity.'

In other words, be there, Amber thought. It was a plain enough directive and, although he couldn't force her to go, she knew she would feel his disapproval and his disappointment if she did not. The only other social events at which her presence was obligatory were departmental sherry parties in the staff common-room, which *she* organised, so this politely worded command said a good deal about Lucas Tremayne's standing at Westbury. Against all the odds, he had carved himself a niche and fitted into it.

And now, since there was no escape short of a con-venient attack of bubonic plague, she began to view the coming Saturday with considerable trepidation, and much reluctance. For a start, there was no way she was going to take Kate along, thrust her into Luke's company and risk whetting their curiosity about each other. That would be asking for trouble. Amber went to see Lucy and asked if she wouldn't mind having Kate on Saturday evening.

'Need you ask? Of course I wouldn't,' her friend replied promptly. 'She might as well stay the night. It will save you picking her up late, and she's always down here Sunday mornings, anyhow.'

Amber listened carefully for any echo of doubt in Lucy's voice, and finding none she ventured tenta-tively, 'It's good of you. After all, it *is* a Saturday evening, and——'

Lucy laughed heartily, a large sound from such a small-boned, silvery lady, and tapped her leather boot with her whip.

'You mean, Tom?' she said, unabashed. 'Don't worry, Kate won't be interrupting anything. He's taking the new stallion to some breeder over Hereford way, and won't be back until Monday. Good thing, too—I could do with a rest!'

Amber coughed and half choked over her coffee.

'Lucy—the things you say sometimes!' she murmured, but her friend did not even blush.

'Why not? We're both mature women, who know what it's about, and I'm here to tell you there's not a lot to choose between Tom and that stallion of his! A girl needs a rest now and then.'

She cocked an eye at Amber, and said mischievously, 'Mind you, they do say a change is as good as a rest, and you, my dear, have the opposite problem. Any chance of your meeting someone interesting at this party?'

Amber looked sharply at her.

'Not you, too! Kate was nattering on a while ago about my needing a boyfriend, and both of you are way off beam,' she stated firmly. 'That's one complication my life can do without.'

'Amber—it's five years since Lawrence died, and you can correct me if I'm wrong, but you've choked off everything male that's even looked at you, so far as I know,' she said gently. 'It just isn't natural to live like that, and I'm not talking only about sex, although to me that's important, but about affection, tenderness, sharing. You can't cut yourself off from human experience for ever.'

'I have Kate. And my job. And I'm trying, in whatever spare moments I can snatch, to write a book,' Amber said stubbornly. 'I can't take any more on board.'

'So you say, but I reckon a romantic fling with a dishy man would do you a power of good,' Lucy persisted. 'What about this Lucas Tremayne? By all accounts, he's a ladies' man. The ride with him would be worth the fall.'

'Heaven forbid!' Amber exclaimed, with such vehemence that her friend started. More calmly, she tried to explain herself. 'I don't think you'd have a romantic fling with Luke Tremayne. You'd probably have your heart well and truly laid waste. Anyhow, why should someone like that ever look at me? He'll probably have some female coming up from London for the occasion.'

Lucy considered this for a moment.

'You underestimate yourself. And you may be wrong—there's been nothing in the gutter Press about him recently, not since that business with the actress who starred in his film. Now, let's see—what are you going to wear? Why don't you treat yourself and buy something new?'

Amber sighed—it was impossible to prevent Lucy from seeing any new man in the locality as an opportunity for her.

'Not a chance. There were the jodhpurs, remember, and Kate has to have new shoes for school. The car's due for servicing, too, and it never comes back from the garage for less than eighty pounds, even if nothing major needs fixing,' she said.

'I know, it's a bore,' Lucy agreed sympathetically. 'I've got it—are you still a size twelve? You never look any fatter to me. There's a green silk thing hanging in my wardrobe that I hardly ever wear—the colour does nothing for me, but on you it'd be terrific. Oh, come on, Amber!' she pressed on, overriding her friend's resistence. 'It's not even a favour, *everyone* swaps clothes. You're taller than I am, but the skirt is a little on the long side anyhow.'

Amber went home with a willing baby-sitter arranged and clutching a plastic bag which contained a jade green skirt and matching top. All she had to do now was endure the party, and although it was silly, she knew, she could not help thinking back to that other occasion when she had been among a group of people at Luke Tremayne's temporary residence.

It had been the day after their lunch at the *auberge*, and the afternoon when he had made love to her by the pool. 'I'll call you,' he had said, when he'd left her at the hotel the previous day, but by lunchtime he hadn't, and Amber was too young and impatient to play a waiting game. She loved him, he was her lover, but something about his manner when they had parted had made her uneasy, and desperately in need of reassurance.

She had taken her bike on the bus as far as Les Eyzies, and ridden it the rest of the way to the farmhouse. Her heart had thumped with the heady anticipation of seeing him again, of being held in his arms, but as she wheeled her machine up the drive she became aware that there were two cars parked alongside the Jaguar.

There were voices, too. Amber came to an abrupt halt, transfixed by the scene in front of her. Chairs and tables had been pulled out from the house on to the weed-filled, overgrown terrace. Bottles of wine stood open, there was crusty bread, bowls of chunky pâté, big wedges of creamy Brie and orange-skinned Port Salut cheese. Much clinking of glasses and chatter. A petite woman with brilliant strawberry-blonde hair was laughing up at a small, wiry, energetic middle-aged man in dark spectacles, a couple were engaged in a vociferous literary discussion in French, and a big, broad-shouldered man was pouring brandy into a punchbowl. Everyone wore bright, casual, but very fashionable clothes, and talked very loudly.

Into this sophisticated little tableau stumbled Amber, in denim shorts and a skimpy cotton T-shirt, wheeling her bike, her mass of curls whipped into a frenzy by the effort of cycling in hot weather, her forehead and palms sticky with the same heat.

It all went suddenly very quiet, and they turned as one and looked at this dishevelled intruder on their gay little party. Amber blanched with embarrassment beneath her tan, and wished she could vanish into the ground. What *was* going on? And where *was* Luke? she wondered, panic-stricken.

And then she saw him. He emerged from the dark, shuttered interior of the house, brandishing a champagne bottle aloft in one hand, his other arm draped casually around the shoulders of a cool, elegant young woman with a short, immaculate cap of blonde hair, wearing a softly draped dress of palest lemon.

'Still collecting strays, Luke?' she asked, in a perfectly modulated voice bearing just a hint of mockery. 'Who's this, then? Is she looking for the Wizard of Oz?'

Luke was looking at Amber as if she were the last person he had expected to see. And perhaps she was, since he hadn't invited her, and he was all too obviously occupied with guests who *were* welcome. Amber swallowed hard, trying to conceal her dismay. He didn't even look like the strange, restless but thoughtful man who had held her in his arms yesterday. If the bottles were anything to go by, a considerable quantity of wine had been consumed, he was laughing and full of *bonhomie*, the perfect host, the life and soul of the party. She was not wanted here.

'I'm sorry!' she gasped. 'I didn't know you had visitors. I'll go.'

'No—please.' He released the blonde woman, crossed the terrace quickly and turned her around again. 'Don't do that—it's a long ride, and you look bushed.'

He led her on to the terrace and introduced her around. 'My agent, Granville Stark, and his wife Clarissa . . .' This was the man in dark glasses and the merry, red-haired woman. 'Malcolm Grant, director of Atkinson and Grant, who are publishing my first novel in the autumn,' this the large man presiding over the punchbowl. 'Jacques Lefèvre from their French subsidiary, and his wife Clemence——' Amber smiled wanly at the French couple. 'Oh, and this is Paula Stanley, my publisher's editor, who guides me along the paths of fiction.'

It was not lost on Amber that he left this introduction until last, and there had to be something significant in that surely. She did not miss, either, the look the blonde woman gave him, tender, knowing, slightly arch, the look a woman turns on a man she loves and knows well.

But it can't be—he loves *me*, Amber wanted to cry. There was nothing in his manner, however, which indicated to her or to anyone else that this was so. Recovered from the surprise of her arrival, he was affable, friendly, pouring her a glass of wine and pressing her to have something to eat, for all the world like an indulgent uncle with a teenage niece. No hint, even in his eyes, of the passionate kisses and caresses of yesterday, the naked, burning embrace and the ardent, irresistible coupling. It might never have taken place.

She remembered now that Granville Stark, Luke's agent, had been kind to her, offering a seat and chatting to her, which helped lessen the terrible alienation which had overcome her. She might have liked him and his laughing, red-haired wife, if she had not been feeling so awful. But for the most part there was a lot of literary backchat, most of which went over the top of Amber's head since it concerned events and personalities unknown to her. Occasionally Luke would smilingly translate an allusion for her, and she smiled too, pretending this was all great fun, and that she was happy with her part in it. And all the while the sleekly elegant Paula was at Luke's side, limpet-like, threading her arm possessively through his, smiling up at him and whispering in his ear some private joke only he could appreciate.

Amber waited, waited for the horror to end, for all these people to leave, so that he and she could be back where they were yesterday, in the enchanted world which had begun by the pool. But it did not happen and, she realised, was not going to happen. Finally, she reached the inescapable solution that she was the one who should leave.

Of course—embarrassingly—she wanted to go to the bathroom first, and Luke directed her inside, pointing her way along a dim corridor. It was as she was about to emerge once more that she heard a low-voiced argument going on at the other end of the corridor, in the kitchen.

'Be reasonable, Paula.' Luke's voice, firm but pleasant. 'I have to drive Amber back to her hotel.'

'Luke—please!' Paula's now, throaty and pleading, but with irritation threaded through it. 'I haven't seen you for a month, and you have to go charging off, just because some ridiculous child lands herself on your doorstep——'

'Hardly a child.' There was a touch of amusement about this, and Amber stepped back, holding her breath, knowing she should either retreat or make her presence known, and able to do neither.

'Well, little more,' Paula said disparagingly. 'Can't she go on her bike? We're never alone, Luke. I know Granville and Clarissa had to come, but why Malcolm had to tag along, bringing that boring Frenchman and his awful wife——'

'Paula!' Luke laughed reprovingly. 'Sh! You're talking about your boss. Have some discretion.'

Something else crept into her voice, sending shivers of recognition down Amber's spine.

'That isn't what you said in Paris.'

'Isn't it?' He was teasing her—or was he? It was hard to tell. 'I can't remember. In Paris I was very seldom sober.'

'Luke, you're impossible. How Gemma ever knew where she was with you, I'll never know!' Amazing as it seemed, there was a tremor in that cool voice.

'Gemma knew perfectly well where she was with me, because she had more sense than to crowd me.' His voice was hard, flat and firm.

'You mean she turned a blind eye to your affairs?' Paula was beginning to sound shrill now, then suddenly her resistance collapsed. 'Luke, I'm sorry, I'm not trying to crowd you. It's just that . . .'

'Paula.' Somehow he had silenced her. Was it just the commanding note in his voice, or was he kissing her? Amber could not see, and dared not emerge from her concealment, but there was a long pause before he said, 'I'm going to take Amber home now, and then I'll be back. All right? Keep the champagne cold and everyone amused. It won't take me long.'

In a few moments and a few words he had destroyed Amber's bright new world. Luke did not love her. He had wanted only to possess her body, briefly, and use it—that was why he had been so troubled to learn she had been a virgin, because he was afraid she would take the experience seriously, as he had not.

It would seem there was already a woman in his life—Paula. And before her there had been Gemma, she who had briefly disturbed his sleep by the pool, but little else, it appeared, since she had turned a blind eye to his affairs. Affairs? How many women did this man keep on a string? Could any woman trust him? And she—stupid, foolish, ignorant—had gladly given herself to him, believing he cared for her.

She took a deep breath and drew back her shoulders before marching out on to the terrace where he was waiting to take her back to her hotel.

The only way she could escape from this with any dignity, any remnant of respect for her own worth, would be to make it clear that yesterday's episode was as meaningless to her as it was to him.

# CHAPTER FIVE

'Yoiks!' Kate chortled gleefully, on learning she was to spend Saturday night at Lucy's. 'I'll be able to start riding earlier on Sunday morning. Super!'

Seeing her mother's rueful smile, she added quickly, 'I hope you enjoy the party, Mum. I mean...you wouldn't want *me* there, would you? It's for...it's for...'

'Old fogies?' Amber suggested sweetly. Sometimes she suspected Kate would rather be at Lucy's than at home; other times, she was sure of it!

'I wasn't going to say that,' Kate said haughtily, and Amber gave her daughter's rump a friendly slap, on passing.

'No, you were only thinking it! Don't worry—I'm sure we fogies will manage to pass on an hour or so without you, and you're right. I doubt anyone your age will be there.'

The house seemed very quiet after she had driven over and deposited Kate at Lucy's, returning alone. She had more than enough time to take a shower and get ready, time that lay heavy on her hands. She did not need to cook herself a meal, there would be plenty to eat at the party. About to make herself some coffee, she changed her mind and did something that was unusual for her. Fishing out the depleted, long-untouched bottle of whisky from the cupboard, she poured herself a stiff double measure, sank into a chair, kicking off her shoes, and took a long, deep swallow.

It was silly to have to resort to artificial courage simply to go to a party given by a man she had believed herself in love with, so long ago that it could almost have happened to someone else, and after she had finished the drink Amber could not say whether she felt better or worse.

She went upstairs, undressed and turned on the shower, running the jets very fiercely and coldly to bring her back to her senses, then padding, naked, into her bedroom to stand thoughtfully in front of her mirror.

It must be the drink. Five years of being alone, five years of marriage to Lawrence and it was Luke's hands she imagined, running over the still taut smoothness of her stomach, sliding beneath her armpits and cupping her breasts... She closed her eyes and groaned, trying to dispel by wishing the physical reactions of her body to the mere thought. It could not be possible that she still wanted him that way. Then why was she experiencing sensations which had not troubled her for years?

Quickly, she slipped into her underclothes and pulled on a pair of tights before climbing into the jade green two-piece. Only then did she risk another look at her reflection, and had to admit Lucy had been right. That deep shade of green was good on her, highlighting the creamy pallor of her skin and the dark, coppery sheen of her hair. Brushing up its heavy weight from the nape of her neck, she anchored the top tresses with pins, but was unable to do anything about the recalcitrant side pieces which framed her face and neck in unruly tendrils. The result was decidedly sexy, and she sucked in her breath, wondering whether she dared let loose this houri, in place of the Amber everyone knew.

But, having put on the clothes and done the hair, there was no sense in spoiling the effect with half-measures. She applied her make-up carefully, swishing blusher over her already high cheekbones, and finishing what was left of the green eyeshadow someone had given her several Christmases ago. A pair of rather barbaric dangling ear-rings—only gold-plate, but none the less effective—finished the picture, and she hoped she hadn't gone over the top.

Wandering downstairs, she pulled a face at herself in the hall mirror, giggled and poured herself another drink. Only a small one this time, but it was as well she wasn't planning to drive. Cal was picking her up, along with the girl from Social Studies he was taking as his guest, who, he said gleefully, never drank anything stronger than fizzy orange, which left him free to imbibe as much as he chose.

Amber wandered aimlessly about the cottage in her stockinged feet, now and then sipping at her drink. She wasn't a drinker, apart from the odd glass of wine, and knew it was not too sensible to go to a party already slightly oiled, so to speak. Nor was the intention working too well because, although it gave her confidence a temporary boost, it did not douse the memories which crowded in on her, thick and fast . . .

Driving back from Tarsac to the hotel at La Roque Gageac again, for the last time, sitting tight-lipped and frozen at Luke's side, trying to hold in the pain so it did not break out and engulf her.

'I said I'd call you, and I would have, you know,' he said quietly, with a touch of reproof. 'I didn't know

Granville et al would turn up today, although I was expecting him and Clarissa some time. After all, I'd borrowed their car.'

This jerked her briefly from her self-absorbed misery.

'It isn't yours?'

'This? No, I'm not in the Jaguar earnings bracket yet,' he said amusedly. 'I'm just a news hack, you know. Maybe one day, if my novel makes it...anyhow, we were all in Paris talking publishing deals, and I wanted to take off for a few weeks, so Granville lent me his car. Paula offered to drive him down so he could pick it up—he and Clarissa are off to Italy. I don't know what plans Malcolm and the Lefèvres have.'

Which made it plain that Luke would be going back to England with Paula.

'I'm sorry I barged in,' Amber said lamely.

'That's all right. You couldn't have known,' he said. 'It was only a very informal, alfresco party. No harm done.' His voice changed suddenly, deepened and became more serious. 'I wish I could say the same about yesterday.'

'You can, can't you?' Amber tried to sound light and unconcerned. 'I enjoyed it, and so did you. It was just a bit of fun, wasn't it?'

'Was it?' He glanced swiftly at her. 'Don't pretend you don't know what I'm talking about. Neither of us took any precautions, and I know it was only the once, but—well, these things can happen.'

A cold sweat broke out all over her skin. She honestly had not given that possibility a thought, perhaps because up until an hour ago she had reposed her trust perfectly in Luke, believing that, whatever happened, all would be well, and with him beside her she would be afraid of nothing.

'You think I could be pregnant?' she said in a small, pinched voice. 'It's not . . . it's not very likely, is it?'

'Probably not . . . but one never knows. If you are, Amber . . .' he paused, looked at her again, then returned his attention to the road, 'you can get in touch with me through the *Examiner*'s office in London. I wouldn't let you down.'

For a fleeting moment, hope blazed anew within her.

'You mean . . . if I were having a baby, you'd marry me?' she said hesitantly.

He swerved the Jaguar so violently round the next bend that it all but ran off the road, and she watched his hands grappling expertly with the steering wheel to right it again.

'For heaven's sake, Amber, be sensible!' he exclaimed, aghast. 'That would be madness! You hardly know me, apart from anything else.' She thought he shuddered, as if the mere idea of matrimony were something to be avoided at all costs, and right then she felt so small that she could have disappeared, unseen, down a crack in the road. More calmly he went on, 'There are other ways I could help. Financial support . . . or if you didn't want to go ahead——'

'I could have an abortion,' she said flatly. She still hurt, but the pride which had been unable to prevent her from running shamelessly after him earlier came rushing to her defence now, bringing with it a welcome, cleansing anger. She would never do that, nor would she ever ask for his help, financial, emotional, or otherwise.

'I'll bear that in mind, but it won't be necessary,' she said stiffly. 'And I wouldn't marry you, even if you wanted me to, because ... because I already have a steady boyfriend. We're practically engaged.'

'You are?' She heard the doubting surprise in his voice. 'What does he do, this boyfriend of yours?'

'His name's Lawrence, and he's a history research fellow,' Amber said glibly. That much was true. Lawrence was one of Uncle Selwyn's pet protégés, and it was also true that he had been hanging around her for several months, without receiving too much encouragement.

'Well, well. Who would've thought it? You weren't too faithful to good old Lawrence yesterday, were you?' he said, with the crooked grin she had come to know so well.

'You weren't so faithful to good old Paula, either!' she riposted.

'Paula?' he repeated amusedly, and she wondered why he bothered with the pretence, when it had been perfectly obvious what was going on, even though he didn't know she had overheard their conversation. But they never pursued the subject, because just then fate or providence, or whatever one likes to call the seemingly arbitrary powers that change the course of our lives, took a hand in the proceedings.

Luke was slowing down as he drove through the village, approaching the hotel but on the opposite side of the road. Drawn up outside the hotel itself was Uncle Selwyn's familiar dark blue saloon, and taking a suitcase from the boot was the tall, lanky figure of Lawrence Kingsland!

Amber did not hesitate. This was a gift from heaven, and she could not refuse it. She never knew whether Luke would have believed her face-saving story without the young man's providential appearance.

'It's Lawrence!' she cried, with only partially feigned delight, for at that moment she genuinely was glad to see him. 'Stop the car, Luke, and I'll get out here.'

She opened the door almost before he had stopped, and jumped out, then pulled her bike from the spacious boot.

'Amber——' he said.

'Please—just go, Luke. I don't want him to think—well, you know! He's very jealous,' she said, more prophetically than she knew. With only the most cursory glance to ensure there was no traffic either way, she ran across the road, threw down her bike and flung her arms around the neck of the startled but wholly pleased young man, moulding her slim body to his in a way she had never done before, all the time he had known her. He hesitated only a moment before dropping the suitcase and gathering her up in an eager embrace.

Amber did not look back. After a brief pause, she heard the Jaguar's engine gather power and cruise off smoothly. Her eyes smarted fiercely against Lawrence's shirt, with the anguish of knowing she would never see Luke again, but when he asked curiously, 'Who was that?' she managed to produce the most casual of shrugs.

'Oh, just some English people I met, staying nearby. One of them gave me a lift back from Les Eyzies. Come on—let's go find Uncle Selwyn.'

And that, thought Amber, sipping her drink and waiting for Cal to arrive, had been the end of that, so far as she and Luke were concerned. Uncle Selwyn was fond of Lawrence, had thought it a good idea if the young research fellow came back with him for the rest of the holiday, and was pleased to see the two young people spending so much time together. He began to look on them as an established couple, and when on their return to England Amber had discovered she was pregnant, it never occurred to him to suspect anyone else could be the father.

'You'll only hurt him more if you tell him the truth, whatever the truth is,' Lawrence had said shrewdly. 'All right, he's shocked and disapproving, but he knows me, likes me, and even a bachelor of his age is aware that young couples occasionally jump the gun. Let him think it—I don't mind.'

'But *I* do,' Amber had protested. 'It's not fair on you. Uncle Selwyn will expect you to do the decent thing and marry me. I have to tell him that's not on!'

'Why not, Amber?' He had put a finger over her lips to silence her. 'It's what I want, too, what I always wanted. I was only waiting until you were a little older, hoping that you'd come to feel the same way.'

'Lawrence, I'm carrying another man's child,' she had reminded him soberly. 'I can't and won't tell you who he is, and there's no chance of his marrying me, but it wasn't . . . I mean, I really loved him. How can I marry you on those terms? It wouldn't be right.'

'I know that you must have loved him, Amber. You aren't the kind of girl who would do that with just anyone. But I love *you*. I'd rather have you this way, than anyone else. Maybe you'll grow to love me in time, and we could make a good life together—have other children of our own.'

When she had remained doubtful, he had produced the clinching argument.

'What else will you do? You can't go to university now, and it will be hard on your uncle's reputation, having an unmarried mother under his roof.'

There was no denying the hard truth of that. A month later they were married, and shortly afterwards they moved to Westbury to start a new life in fresh surroundings.

All the lights were ablaze in the house by the river when they drove up, but to Amber it still had a sepulchral air about it. Only someone utterly devoid of imagination could live there and be unaware of that aura of ill-being, she thought, and Luke surely did not fit that description. She still did not fully understand why he had been so insistent on moving in.

He met them at the door.

'Welcome to Tremayne's Folly,' he said airily, leading them through the hall. 'Why, Amber,' he whispered in her ear, 'what have you done to yourself? You look like something from the cover of *Cosmopolitan*!'

Amber had already begun to regret the too low *décolletage* Lucy had insisted was perfect on her. 'If you've got it, flaunt it!'

'But I haven't got enough of it,' she had protested, and Lucy had shaken her head firmly.

'Nonsense! Maybe you'll never make Page Three, but what you *have* got is in pretty good shape!'

But on this warm summer evening the big, well-proportioned reception room was full of women with bare shoulders and plunging necklines, so she certainly did not look out of place—just not her normal, comfortable, everyday self.

Luke wore a casual suit with a fashionably unstructured jacket of mid-grey slubbed silk, which must have cost a mint, she reckoned, realising that it was the first time she had ever seen him dressed up for an evening occasion. He pressed a glass of white wine into her hand and led her towards the buffet table which was laden with trays of canapés and cold cuts, wafer-thin smoked salmon, gâteaus and cakes of all kinds.

'I hope you're going to eat something. I've been slaving in the kitchen all day,' he said sternly.

Maybe it was the whisky she had already drunk, but Amber found an unusual recklessness invading her.

'Liar. You've had the caterers in,' she retorted, smiling.

'You've found me out, as usual,' he admitted cheerfully.

Her eyes scanned the room, separating the familiar people from those who were strangers to her, a fairly even number of each being present. As yet, the two groups were not mingling very much. Amber was introduced to two well-known newspaper columnists, a lady novelist with a reputation for outrageous behaviour, and an American film producer, before she found herself thankfully occupying a secluded corner with Gerald Courtney.

'What strange people Luke seems to know,' he observed.

'They're probably saying the same thing about us,' she laughed, and he glanced oddly at her.

'My dear Amber—what a peculiar thing to say. What could possibly be strange about *us*?'

'Not a thing, Gerald,' she agreed weakly. She was on to her second glass of wine, and it was reacting unpredictably against the whisky, giving her a light-headed, floating feeling. She bit into a vol-au-vent, deciding it would be a good idea to eat a little and not have anything else to drink, at least for a while.

She was over at the buffet table helping herself to canapés when she turned around and came face to face with Granville Stark. The sudden shock cleared her head of the floating sensation at a stroke, and with this new clarity came a realisation of how dense she had been. It had honestly never occurred to her that she might meet someone she had come across before—someone who was not promised to discretion, as Luke was. Someone who might circulate and pass on the interesting information that Mrs Kingsland and Mr Tremayne were not exactly strangers to one another!

She stared at him for a long beat, in horrified silence, and then he said amiably, 'Hello—I'm Granville Stark, Luke's agent. Are you one of the boffins from the university?'

He didn't know her! Amber breathed again, thanking the years, the neckline and the upswept hair.

'Not really,' she said. 'I'm just the departmental secretary.'

'That sounds like a handful of a job to me,' he said. 'If you ever tire of it, come to London and work for me. I can't seem to keep a good secretary for five minutes. They all go to America sooner or later—for the money.'

'I imagine your line of work would be extremely interesting,' she said. 'Looking after writers, I mean.'

He pulled a wry face.

'It is. I hold their hands, nurse their egos, negotiate their contracts, celebrate their successes and support them through their failures—and take ten per cent of every penny they earn,' he said. 'But for every big earner like Luke, there are hundreds struggling along, so I don't make a lot from all my clients. The talent lies in spotting the right potential at the beginning. It isn't always easy to tell who will make it.'

'Was it easy with Luke?' she asked curiously.

Granville Stark spread out his hands.

'Yes and no. He was already an established journalist, of course, but they don't always make the best writers of fiction. He had something to say, and a need to get it down on paper, but he also had an alarming tendency towards self-destruction in those early days. He seems to have worked that through his system now, fortunately, although he'll probably always gravitate towards danger.'

A tendency towards self-destruction? Amber recalled fleetingly the reckless, restless man she had met in France, a hard-drinking individual driven by sudden swings of mood, who took and discarded women with cavalier unconcern. For the first time it occurred to her to look behind the easily visible façade, seeking reasons for his behaviour. Maybe Granville Stark could tell her more about Luke, and what made him tick. But why should he? Perhaps he already felt he had said enough, for he changed the subject abruptly.

'Fascinating house, this, isn't it? But then, Luke does have a penchant for choosing interesting places to live.'

Amber's pulse began to thump unsteadily, because from there it was only a short jump to Tarsac and her own dishevelled appearance there, and she wondered faintly if he would make the connection. But at that very moment Luke appeared beside them.

'Come and have a look at the river from the window,' he said, putting an arm around Amber's shoulder. 'Excuse us, Granville—you've already seen the view, haven't you?'

It was still daylight, but the dark turbulence of the waters made one think of blackest night.

'Ugh!' Amber said, gazing down. 'I don't know how you can bear to live here, Luke. It would give me the creeps. Do I really have to look at this?'

'No,' he said. 'But you were looking a little uneasy, so I thought I'd better rescue you from Granville. Although you needn't have worried, your past is safe from him. He can identify any published writer from a line of their prose, but he's hopeless with faces. Clarissa might have recognised you, but she's in Australia, visiting her sister. I'm not so sure you'll fool Paula—she's pretty sharp.'

'Paula!' Amber cried, alarmed. She had thought of the blonde woman as another episode in Luke's saga of women, a figure from his past, never expecting her to surface tonight. 'She isn't here—is she?'

'No, but she will be,' he said. 'She's driving down from Scotland. She's my editor, Amber,' he told her. 'She was assigned to me when I was first published by Atkinson and Grant, when she was new to the company. Now she's one of their senior editors, and I——'

'You're the jewel in their crown,' Amber finished.

'I wouldn't put it quite so strongly,' he said modestly. 'My first novel was really only a *succès d'estime*—good reviews and not a lot of cash. But the second one hit it big, and now they are hoping I'll deliver with the third. It's a tall order, trying to repeat a success; harder, I think, than trying to achieve it in the first place. Sometimes, I wonder——'

She never did find out what it was he wondered, because he steered the conversation away from himself, quite suddenly.

'Cal tells me you write a little.'

Amber stifled a groan, wishing her colleagues would not be quite so free with such information—an unreasonable wish, she knew, since she had never made any secret of it, working every day in an environment peopled with inveterate scribblers.

'"A little" is the phrase,' she said dismissively, not really wanting to talk about it to this assured, established author. 'The odd short story, and a novel I keep taking in and out of a drawer. I don't have a lot of time.'

'Haven't you ever tried to publish—or at least get an opinion? Or are you afraid to?' He laughed at her offended expression. 'Don't be ashamed to admit it—*all* writers are paranoid about rejection.'

'Even you?' she asked, disbelievingly.

'Even me. It never leaves you, however successful you become, I promise you. But if you're seriously trying, I could help you, if you wanted me to.'

'You?' She stiffened involuntarily, remembering the promise she had made herself years ago, never to seek any kind of assistance from this man. What she wrote was precious to her, in a special way, just as Kate was,

and she could not help feeling that anything of hers
that Luke Tremayne touched, he would destroy.

He shrugged, almost diffidently.

'Well—Granville would, if I asked him to. He could
run an eye over your work and tell you if you had
any possibilities, or should go away and take up
French knitting instead. If you really do want to be
a writer, that is, as opposed to just cherishing a
pretence that you do, which is not uncommon.'

And this, she recognised, was yet another challenge. Dared she accept it, and risk being told that
the talent she thought she had was insufficient? Damn
him for putting her in a position where she had to
make the choice, for coming back and creating all
kinds of turmoil in her quiet life!

'I'll think about it,' she said.

'Do that. And think about something else,' he advised wryly. 'When Paula turns up, do you want me
to have a quiet word in her ear, ask her to pretend
she's never met you before? I'll have to tell her why,
of course—she's a very inquisitive lady—about
our...affair...which you, for reasons best under
stood by yourself, are anxious to keep quiet.'

She had the uncomfortable but quite definite feeling
that, once again, he was trying to put her on the spot.

'No!' she said swiftly. 'Don't tell her that. She
probably won't recognise me. I only met her briefly,
and it was a long time ago. Why should she?'

'As you please.' He shrugged again. 'I honestly can't
see why it should matter, Amber, if all the world knew
we were once lovers.'

Amber could not say, It matters because people will
talk. They'll talk about you and me, about Kate,
they'll put dates and times and ages together, and

whispers will start going around. She had told him categorically that Kate was nine, gambling that her daughter's age was unlikely to be a subject of discussion between him and any of her colleagues. Why should it be? But it might, if they learned anything about her past association with Luke. This was one cat that needed to be kept firmly in the bag, with the string securely tied.

'Luke . . . not to put too strong an interpretation on it, you have a certain . . . shall we say . . . reputation?' she said. 'In a short time you will be gone from Westbury. As you say, you are just passing through. I, on the other hand, have to live, work and bring up my child right here. I can do without that kind of scandal hanging over me.'

He looked at her, long, hard and, she thought, with a certain amount of distaste.

'I couldn't believe, at first, that you were truly so concerned about your lily-white image,' he said cuttingly. 'Maybe one day you'll find the courage to be yourself, and not give a hoot about what people say. Personally, I'm with the Duke of Wellington with regard to scandal—publish and be damned is my reaction. But have it your own way. Meanwhile, you'll just have to take your chances with Paula.'

He turned away, not exactly abandoning her, but in the way one does at parties, casually joining in another passing conversation. But it didn't feel like that to Amber. It felt as if he had quite deliberately washed his hands of her and thrown her to the lions. Stung by his carefully reined disgust, she accepted another glass of wine poured by someone she didn't know, drank it quickly, and didn't refuse a refill, but somehow the reckless, floating, don't-care sensation would not come back.

She saw Paula's arrival from a distance, at the other end of the room. In her mid-thirties, Luke's editor would be now; and the years had not dealt too unkindly with her. She still wore her fine blonde hair short, revealing her pure, elegant profile, she was scarcely less slender, and was certainly as soignée as ever. Amber saw her move into Luke's arms for the casual kiss of welcome which was almost as common as a handshake now, and presumably as meaningless.

But...she did not immediately let go, as was usually the pattern. Her hands clutched his arms, and she clung...yes, that was the word. Her eyes were lifted to his with a kind of mute appeal, and her cheek rested against his for longer than it should have.

In a flash, Amber thought—she still loves him! It wasn't just another of those brief affairs he had become famous for. After ten years, this one was still going on, amazingly, for he had apparently neither married her nor cast her aside. Turning a blind eye? Amber wondered, finding her own hand trembling. Looking the other way...not willingly, she was sure, for she had known long ago that Paula was of a possessive temperament...while he fooled around elsewhere...then taking him back? For all those years?

I couldn't have done that, Amber thought, surprised, for she had never thought of herself as possessive. But this much she knew—she would have had to have all his love, completely, or let him go.

She closed her hand firmly around her glass to keep it still. She'd had a narrow escape long ago, but she had made the right choice. Had he known that he was her child's father, he would have been forever flitting

in and out of her life, constantly making her un-
happy. And, were he to find out now, that could still
happen. Amber faced the stark, brutal truth she could
not avoid—he still had the power to make her un-
happy, even now—or he would, if she gave him the
opportunity.

Glancing out of the window, she saw that it had
gone dark, and this filled her with relief, for it meant
it was sufficiently late for her to make an excuse and
leave. Knowing that Luke would not help her, she cir-
culated as much as she could, keeping an eye on
Paula's progress and covertly avoiding her, making
her way gradually towards the door. There was a telephone in the hall—she'd ring for a taxi.

But, almost as she had her escape route in sight,
she was detained by Sorrel, who was being blatantly
chatted up by the film producer, and seized the opportunity to draw someone else into the conversation.
Amber made polite yes and no replies, and watched
her chance, feeling no obligation to stay—Sorrel was
old enough and sophisticated enough to deal with unwanted Romeos unaided.

'Ronnie,' said a cool, cultured voice behind her, 'I
didn't know you were going to be here. I thought you
were still in Los Angeles.'

'Flew in three days ago,' the film producer said
breezily. 'Paula—what d'you know—this little lady
here is a real live doctor of philosophy! Did ya know
they made 'em that cute?'

Paula was only half listening. She was looking at
Amber, intent but faintly puzzled, her fine eyebrows
slightly drawn together.

'Haven't we met before somewhere?' she asked imperiously, without preamble.

Amber looked back at her, blankly, directly, making a colossal effort not to give herself away by flinching.

'Have we?' she asked doubtfully. 'One meets so many people around, it's difficult to keep track of them all, isn't it? Please excuse me.'

She smiled sweetly and flitted into the hall, hoping that Paula's curiosity was only fleeting, and would soon be distracted by more interesting matters.

Quickly she reached the telephone and dialled the number of a taxi company she often called in the course of her work, but before she made the connection someone's hand forestalled her, took the receiver from her and quietly replaced it.

'What do you think you're doing?' Luke asked, smiling but far from pleased, she could tell.

'I'm phoning for a taxi—or trying to,' she retorted. 'How dare you cut me off? I'll pay for the call, if that's what's bothering you,' she added stupidly.

He ignored this offer, as well he might, she supposed.

'It's only ten-thirty. Why do you have to leave so early?'

'Does it matter? It was good of you to invite me, thank you very much, but now I want to go home,' she replied acerbically. 'I can't drag Cal and his friend away before they're ready to leave, so a taxi seemed the obvious answer.'

'Forget it. If you must go, I'll drive you,' he said, shepherding her towards the door.

'Luke, no! You can't run out on your own party,' she gasped.

'For you, it seems, I can,' he said softly, pointedly. 'I've done as much before. They're all enjoying themselves. There's plenty to eat, drink and gossip about, and they probably won't notice I'm gone. It won't take me long.'

His last words were an exact echo of what he had said on that day when he'd left his guests at the farmhouse to take her back to her hotel. It had to be unconscious, she thought—hadn't it? He could not possibly remember what he had said at the time. But she was so stunned that she let him guide her out and settle her in the car without protest.

It was warm inside the car, and the night outside its windows was velvet dark. Amber leaned back luxuriously. The floating sensation had returned, but now, curiously, it did not worry her. She was relaxed, strangely disembodied, riding through the night like a princess, dressed in whispering silk, and if she looked in a mirror now she would see someone ethereally beautiful, a vision of shimmering femininity. Beside her, jacketless now, his shirt open at the throat, Luke Tremayne, hers again for the duration of the journey, taken from her once by a malicious fate, and temporarily—miraculously—given back.

Did she have to let him go the minute they reached her door?

# CHAPTER SIX

THE JAGUAR eased to a halt outside the cottage. With its lights switched off, everything around was in darkness, only the faint glow illuminating the car's interior.

'Here you are, Cinderella,' he said drily.

Amber smiled slowly, the green eyes slightly narrowed. Several long tendrils of hair had escaped from her topknot, lending her an air of sensuous dishevelment, and the green silk top had slipped from one shoulder, baring an expanse of flesh that gleamed whitely, invitingly. She had no idea how tempting she looked, but she knew he was about to kiss her—knew, and joyfully, brazenly had no intention of protesting.

Her mouth opened willingly under his; she went into his arms as if the interruption of the unexpected guests at the farmhouse, and the years thereafter, had never existed, and they had simply gone on from where they had left off at the pool. She moaned beneath his kisses, throwing back her head and inviting him to explore her throat and neck with his lips, twisting towards him in her seat as his fingers slid caressingly over the bare shoulder, gasping with electric excitement as his hand found its way beneath the thin silk to take possession of her breast.

But it wasn't enough—she wanted more, wanted to be naked with him, to have him inside her, possessing all of her. In five years of marriage she had never once felt like this—only with him, that one, unfor-

gettable time, had she known this sweet, fierce, prim-
itive urge, and then she had been an ignorant girl.
Now she was a woman, who could truly give him back
as much as he gave her.

'Oh, Luke!' she gasped. 'Take me inside. Take
me——'

'Amber,' he said distinctly, in a stern, school-
masterly voice, and although he still held her his hands
were no longer moving over her body, only she was
writhing against him. 'My dear, silly girl—I do believe you've had too much to drink!'

She was still then, as the floating feeling drained
away, leaving her cold and deflated and utterly foolish.

'Come on,' he said indulgently, putting her clothes
to right, opening the car door and helping her out.
'I ought to have known!'

The cool air hit her like a smack in the face as she
got out; she swayed slightly, and he supported her.
She heard him laugh softly, hated him, but could not
find the strength to do anything about it.

'Where are the keys?' he asked, giving her a slight
shake. 'Keys, Amber,' he repeated, as if talking to an
imbecile, very slowly and patiently. 'I can hardly leave
you on the doorstep.'

She fumbled in her handbag, wondering why she
kept so much rubbish in there, why it was taking her
so long to complete this one simple action. Finally she
located them, meekly handing them to him; with one
arm around her waist, he unlocked the door. She felt
herself lifted—very easily, she had not forgotten how
strong he was—and carried up the stairs, but there
was nothing romantic about it. She might as well have
been a sack of potatoes, she thought muzzily, for all
the amorous intent he showed towards her now.

He deposited her on the bed, removed her shoes, and pulled the quilt over her.

'Nothing wrong with you that a good night's sleep won't cure,' he said reassuringly. 'You won't feel like running in the London Marathon tomorrow, but that's by the way. Sleep tight.'

She felt . . . or did she merely imagine . . . his fingers lightly brush her cheek? And then everything was mercifully dark.

When Kate arrived home at lunchtime on Sunday, she could not understand why her mother looked faintly queasy when she asked hungrily what there was to eat.

'Chicken. Can't you smell it cooking?' Amber asked shortly. She certainly could, and the smell had been turning her stomach over for the past hour. Even preparing this meal had been a penance; there was no way she could face eating it. She had a headache, too, thumping away at her left temple, and knew she wasn't going to feel better until she could lie down again and let today pass into oblivion.

But the afternoon brought Lucy, agog to know what the party had been like, who had been there, and if there had been any man worthy of Amber's attention.

Waiting until Kate was out of earshot in the garden, Amber said a little curtly, 'It was all right, I suppose. I think I had a bit too much to drink.'

Lucy chortled with surprised amusement.

'You? But you hardly drink at all!' she exclaimed. 'You poor thing—do you feel fiendish? No wonder Kate said you hadn't eaten any lunch. Now, let's see— you should have a raw egg, beaten up in orange juice, or else a port and brandy. I know lots of super hangover cures, none of which works, so far as I've ascertained.'

'Yuk—as Kate would say!' Amber managed a faint grimace. 'I'd settle for a powder that would make the party never have taken place.'

Lucy's eyes opened wide and eager.

'Why—what happened? Do tell!' she begged.

'At the party? Oh, nothing,' Amber said, truthfully enough. 'I mean, I didn't dance the fandango on the table or anything. I only started to feel weird when I got here.'

That rather glossed over the interlude in Luke's car, but she did not feel like confiding that to Lucy, or to anyone else. It was bad enough that she had behaved like a sex-starved madwoman, going wild under his touch, and virtually begging him to make love to her! It was even worse that at some time in the near future—probably tomorrow—she would have to come face to face with him again, with that scene still fresh in her mind, and most probably in his, too!

'Oh, dear!' Lucy said, crestfallen. 'And here was I expecting some gorgeous hunk—probably Luke Tremayne himself—to sweep you off your feet.'

Amber had to look down. Luke had swept her off her feet, all right, and up to the bedroom, but only because she'd been incapable of getting there under her own stream. *Very* Scarlett O'Hara, she thought ruefully.

'I'm pretty sure he's having an affair with his editor,' she said, thinking that ought to put paid to her friend's unhealthy expectations for herself and Luke. Unfortunately, it involved her in answering more questions, giving a detailed description of Paula, and by the time she left Amber was exhausted. Really,

Lucy was a dear, but not the soul of tact, and she did tire you out!

By Monday morning, Amber's hangover had worn off, and she was physically back to her normal self. But it would have been untrue to say that she felt any better, and every mile of her drive into Westbury might have been a ride in a tumbril towards a waiting guillotine. She could already see in her mind's eye the amused expression on Luke's face, and awaited anxiously the taunting comments he was sure to make about her wanton behaviour on Saturday night.

A glance at the timetable she kept for all members of staff reminded her that Luke was lecturing that morning, but this temporary reprieve only postponed the evil hour that had to come, and she would have much preferred to get it over and done with.

Amber did not know what impulse prompted her to slip quietly into the back of the lecture-room. Perhaps it was some mad notion that she would be better prepared to face him if she saw him first, before he saw her.

Certainly he was unaware of her now, totally absorbed in the group of students and in what he was saying. He was back with Hopkins again, talking quietly but very intently about the 'terrible sonnets' the poet wrote in the last years of his short life. And as he spoke about darkness, alienation, sterility and the failure of his inspiration his listeners could almost imagine that he himself had walked this path, that he knew it very personally and bitterly.

'I wake and feel the fell of dark, not day.
What hours, O what black hours we have spent
This night . . .'

The muted voice dropped the heartfelt words into the utter stillness of the room, and Amber, along with everyone else, held her breath. The desolation reached out, gripped her, and she too, walked through a dark night of the soul, fraught with self-loathing and devoid of all hope.

> '... I see
> The lost are like this, and their scourge to be
> As I am mine, their sweating selves, but worse.'

Amber turned blindly and fled the room, letting the door swing to behind her. She virtually ran along the corridor, and did not stop until she was back in the office, with the door closed behind her.

Something had touched her back there, as she did not want to be touched. Across the intervening space, she had felt Luke's own remembered emotions communicating themselves to her, raw and honest and perfectly recalled, so that she knew that at some time in his life he had felt exactly like that.

She did not *want* to know and sympathise with his past heartaches and sorrows. He had caused her enough of her own, and to admit that he, too, had suffered at some time in his life was to admit his humanity and mitigate his guilt. She could not afford this softening of attitude towards him. It was hard wholly to disapprove of and understand someone at the same time—a mental feat she did not believe she could accomplish.

'Hello.'

He had entered quietly—or was it that she had been too preoccupied? Amber jumped.

'I do wish you wouldn't sneak up on people like that!' she said crossly.

'Would you like me to wear hobnailed boots so you could hear me coming along the corridor?' he asked. The smile that played with the corners of his mouth caused a sudden, wrenching pain deep within her. 'Didn't you enjoy my lecture, Amber?'

'I didn't know you had seen me,' she said, startled.

'I hadn't, until you made your swift, rather dramatic exit. I take it the poetry wasn't to your liking?'

'Oh, yes!' she protested. 'That poem you were reading...it was so...moving, in the most awful way. I hadn't heard it before. Actually, I tried to get a copy of Hopkins from the university library, but they're all out.'

'My students are all reading him,' he said, not without a certain satisfaction in his results. 'I'll lend you mine. It's not the easiest of reading, but well worth the effort, I think.'

He smiled again, briefly, casually, and she saw he was about to leave. Not one word had he said about Saturday night, not even by the merest veiled hint or knowing look had he reminded her of it. It seemed, astonishingly, that he intended to spare her the embarrassment by pretending that nothing had happened.

Absurdly, it was she who could not let it go at that. Unless it was aired, the memory would hang between them, unspoken but not forgotten. And some time, when he was feeling less charitable, she suspected he would fling it in her face. Better to bring it out in the open now.

'Luke—about Saturday night...' she began awkwardly.

'Amber.' He placed a hand over hers, its restraining warmth spreading up her arm until she could feel it near her heart. 'You weren't the first and won't be the last female to have too much tipple, get slightly amorous, and regret it later. I quite understand that it wouldn't have occurred had you been stone-cold sober. Nothing very much happened, anyhow, so don't make a big thing of it. It's forgotten.'

Amber's throat was uncomfortably dry. She should have been grateful to him for this magnanimous attitude, but that brisk, dismissive 'nothing very much happened' stung more deeply than she wanted to admit.

'Well, of course, I know it was nothing to a reputed bedroom athlete such as yourself,' she said sarcastically. 'But I don't make a habit of . . . of . . .'

'Of getting yourself groped in parked cars?' he supplied bluntly. 'What a very sheltered life you must have led, indeed! I would have thought that was part and parcel of twentieth-century courting! Tell me, Amber, are you going to live the rest of your life in nostalgic contemplation of your romantic young marriage, or are you ever going to get out where the action is again?'

Amber flinched so hard that she knew he must have seen her recoil.

'Don't talk about Lawrence and me in that flippant manner!' she snapped back at him. 'He was a good man, and a good husband. He would never have treated women as casually as you seem to think is your right!'

He made not the slightest effort to defend himself on that charge.

'He may indeed have been a cross between Sir Galahad and Robert Redford, for all I know, but he's dead, Amber,' he said brutally. 'You, on the other hand, are still alive, a fact you tend sometimes to forget.'

'You think I should be demonstrating it by going to bed with a different man every night?' Amber flashed scornfully. 'I'm sorry, but I don't find the prospect appealing!'

He considered this for a moment, looking closely at her, the smile spreading slowly across his features.

'No? I thought you were all set to make a start, on Saturday,' he said slyly.

Well, that hadn't taken him long, she thought bitterly. His generosity was certainly short-lived! Amber snatched her hand from beneath his, but his reactions were too quick for her. He seized and held it in a strong, one-handed grip, twisting her towards him.

'Not so fast,' he said, in a dangerously soft voice. 'You liked it well enough at the time, or so I thought.'

His lips brushed her forehead, her cheek and, very lightly, her mouth, and she trembled uncontrollably, hating herself, but unable to conceal that she liked it now. His free hand slid up the smooth white front of her shirt to her breast, teasing it to a hard peak of quivering pleasure. 'You liked this, too, as I remember.'

Amber wrenched herself free, whirling, she got the hard barrier of the desk safely between them.

'Don't you *ever* touch me again, Luke Tremayne!' she spat out, breathing very hard. 'If you can't persuade one of your...your London fancy-pieces to come to Westbury and keep you amused, then find someone else here! The town's full of women—it shouldn't be too difficult!'

He gave a gently amused, quite unabashed smile.

'Amber, if I spent half the time thrashing around in bedrooms that you seem to believe I do, how do you imagine I'd find the opportunity, or have the energy, to write 150,000-word novels and a weekly column for the *Examiner*, notwithstanding the fact that half my life I'm in transit between one place and another, where it's difficult to do more than ogle the stewardesses? Think about it,' he advised mildly. 'You're as obsessed by sex as some tabloid editors I could mention!'

She gave a gasp of outrage.

'I am *far* from obsessed by sex!' she denied furiously. 'I'm not even remotely interested in it!'

'"The lady doth protest too much, methinks,"' he quoted drily. 'You may very well live like a nun, Amber—I'd guess you probably do, but one can be equally obsessive denying something's importance as one can affirming it.'

That left her floundering, for all her anger, for there was just enough unpalatable truth in it to make her uncomfortable, especially when she recalled the strange physical yearnings which had plagued her since he came back into her life.

'Please get out of my office,' she said icily. 'I've work to do, and I've no wish to continue this conversation.'

'Fair enough. I've got better things to do, too,' he said witheringly. 'I'm taking Mrs Grant to lunch, and if I'm not mistaken, she's waiting for me in the quadrangle.'

Amber could not prevent herself from glancing curiously out of the window. There, pacing a little impatiently along the path beneath the flowering trees, she saw the slender, unmistakable figure of a woman in a softly elegant summer suit of palest lilac, her hair a shimmering golden cap.

'That's Paula,' she said, puzzled.

'It is, indeed,' he agreed smoothly. 'Mrs Malcolm Grant, no less. Didn't I tell you? It must have slipped my mind. She married him, five years ago.'

She was speechless as he left the office, and was still standing rigidly in the same position when he popped his head back round the door.

'Oh, I forgot—have a nice day,' he said cheerily, before disappearing again.

For a long time, Amber could not return her proper concentration to her work. She was thoroughly sickened by what she had just heard from Luke's own lips. Paula Stanley... Mrs Grant, to address her correctly... was a married woman. What was more, she was married to Malcolm Grant, who had had faith in Luke long ago, as a new novelist, and had helped steer his literary career in the right direction.

But loyalty, decency, all those normal human considerations, did not apply to Luke Tremayne. Why should they? He was a free spirit, above such trivia, and if he wanted to carry on a long-standing affair with his publisher's wife, who was also his own editor, why, then that was exactly what he did.

That morning, Amber had felt like one who stands at a partly open door, catching a tantalising glimpse of what lay beyond, but unable to see the room in its entirety. What she had strained to see was Luke's inner self, in which all his behaviour must have its roots. 'I wake and feel the fell of dark . . .'

But now, she no longer cared, or wanted to know any more about those inner springs. This man quite simply did not care who he hurt, who he betrayed. He lived as he chose, believing his God-given talent was enough justification for his existence, and gave him ample excuse to tread over the rights and feelings of others. Why should she care about any suffering he had endured? He had more than deserved it, whatever it was.

That evening, after Kate had gone to bed, Amber had had every intention of attacking a pile of mending she had been putting off for some time—buttons that needed sewing on, hems that required turning up, jeans with holes in, long overdue for patching.

Instead, she could not have said why, she gravitated towards the Victorian desk she had rescued from a junk shop and lovingly restored to polished beauty, and took out her long-unfinished novel.

She knew all too well that, writing only intermittently, as she did, she lacked the flow, the assured continuity of the writer who sits down every day with the story and characters fresh in his or her mind from the day before. She had to pick up the threads and knit them together; it was half an hour of pen-chewing and head-scratching for every laborious page, and by midnight tiredness would have put paid to creativity. But there was no other way, so she slogged on, and was just beginning to warm to her theme when a knock at the door disturbed her.

She glanced at the old brass ship's clock on the wall. It was after ten—who would call at this time, unexpectedly? Conscious of her situation as a woman alone with a child, she left the chain on the door as she cautiously opened it an inch.

'You can raise the portcullis and lower the drawbridge,' said Luke Tremayne. 'My intentions are not dishonourable—well, not more than usual.'

Amber released the chain, half reluctantly. There was a suffocating tightness in her chest, and she only gestured but did not speak as she invited him in.

'I brought the copy of Hopkins, while I remembered it, since I won't be in the university tomorrow. I have to go up to town for a few days.'

Amber knew that 'town' could only mean London.

'With Paula?' she asked, trying to sound casual.

'No, Paula left this afternoon, she has an early meeting tomorrow,' he replied easily. 'She gave Granville a lift, as he'd come up by train, and she had her car.'

Oh, who are you fooling? Amber wanted to say, I understood you didn't give a damn what anyone thought. But of course this lady had a husband, who was also his publisher, so in this case, he, too, was bound by convention to be discreet. Paula stayed the weekend, so did Granville, to make it all seem respectable—business colleagues at a houseparty! You're a hypocrite, Luke Tremayne, she thought with bitter amusement.

He had caught sight of her open desk, and smiled.

'That I approve of—a lady with a writing desk in her kitchen. I'm sorry if I interrupted your work.'

Amber affected a shrug of unconcern.

'It doesn't matter. I wasn't getting on any too well,' she admitted. But something in her voice must have betrayed her deeper dissatisfaction. He put down the slim volume of poetry on the pine kitchen table, dug his hands deep in his pockets, and regarded her with thoughtful sympathy.

'Amber, we all have days like that, when nothing jells, and we doubt our own powers. And you—well, you're up against it. You have a job and a family which demand all your time and attention. You're trying to work when you're most tired, at your lowest ebb. The best advice anyone could give you, if you're really serious about writing, is give up the job—for a while, at least.'

It was realistic counsel, she knew, from one who did not know her circumstances. She shook her head, unsure how to answer without giving herself away. But, meeting his all too perceptive eyes, she realised she had not fooled him for very long.

'You can't, can you?' he said. 'I had it all wrong, before. You really do need the money.'

There was not much sense in persisting with a pretence he had already seen through.

'Is it so obvious?' she said, attempting a feeble joke. 'Am I *that* threadbare?'

'Threadbare?' he repeated, with a sharp laugh. 'No, Amber, far from it. You're always immaculately turned out, even if you can't keep that hair of yours under control! You've got instinctive, if rather individual style, and it shows. But I'm a trained observer, I get around among all kinds of people and know the price of all kinds of commodities. For one thing, you'd have changed your car years ago, if you could have.'

'And there are worn patches on my carpet,' she said wryly. 'All right, Luke—I've a mortgage and a daughter, and I can't afford to let up.' Defiance edged her voice. 'I can't be the only woman in that situation.'

'No, but . . .' He hesitated, still looking so directly into her eyes that she was unable to break her gaze away. 'I know this is really none of my business, but...surely your husband's life insurance would have provided for you? Don't tell me he didn't think about such things?'

Amber sighed.

'He did, of course. But the premium was due just before he died, and...and somehow, he forgot to post it.' She did not add that they'd had a furious row that morning when he'd rushed out, to be killed in a collision with a motor-cyclist making an ill-advised right turn. 'So we weren't covered, and not surprisingly, the insurance company wouldn't pay up.'

Luke whistled and shook his head.

'Amber, that's rough! I'd wondered, of course, but I didn't know about the insurance business. What about your Uncle Selwyn? Didn't he help you out?'

It was funny, but the reaction she might have expected to feel on touchy subjects like her personal finances did not occur. Instead of bristling and telling him to mind his own damn business, she felt something close to relief in telling him about it. The fact that she didn't understand this sudden need and ability to confide in him did not render it less so.

'Uncle Selwyn was very kind—he helped me and Kate in a lot of ways, as much as I would let him,' she admitted, switching on the kettle automatically and fetching cups from the cupboard. 'I was a bit . . . well, stiff-necked about accepting help in those days, determined to be independent, etc, etc.'

'I can imagine,' Luke murmured with a smile. 'Battling Amber, bent on playing the Lone Ranger, eh?'

'Something like that.' She returned the smile carefully, wary of this odd new rapport which surely could not bode any good for her. 'Uncle said it didn't really matter, as most of his money would come to me in the long run, anyhow, but I didn't think about that. He was getting on, but he seemed fit, and I thought he'd probably live to see Kate's children! Then he went—just like that. Coronary thrombosis.'

She made the coffee, added milk and sugar, and pushed a cup towards him.

'And?' Luke prompted gently. 'What *did* happen to the money he'd left you?'

'Oh . . .' She pushed a nervous hand through the feathery tendrils of dark red hair. 'There was some confusion about his will. He'd made some amendments, but hadn't let his solicitor have it back, and no one could find it in the house. He was getting a bit absent-minded, you know—probably threw it out with the Sunday papers.' She gave a brittle laugh. 'His sister claimed most of his estate from an old will dating from before he adopted me. She never approved of his doing that.'

'You could have contested,' Luke said, and she shook her head vigorously.

'I know, that's what the solicitor said, but it would have cost money to fight it through the courts, and I might not have won in the end. Besides, I didn't want any unpleasantness. Uncle Selwyn gave me a home and brought me up. I didn't reckon he owed me any more. I was young and healthy, and capable of earning my keep. I still am——' She forced a grin. 'Well, relatively so.'

'My dear Amber, you're in the prime of your womanhood, and don't let anyone tell you other wise,' he said, very softly. 'I could persuade you of it very easily, if you would only let me.' His eyes explored her face, her hair, the curves of her body, as if his hands were longing to do the same, and she stiffened.

'Luke, please, I told you——'

'I know, you're not interested in that kind of thing,' he said. 'Why don't I believe you? Probably because your words are saying one thing, and your body quite another. OK!' He threw up both hands, as if fending off an attack. 'I'll be good. If I can't be any service to you that way, at least fish out those short stories and let me give them to Granville while I'm in London.'

Amber sat still for several seconds, weighing up this offer and deciding whether to take advantage of it. Finally, she admitted to herself that the time had come when she must find out if she had any real ability at all. She could not turn her back on this challenge. Getting up, she took the pages of typescript from her desk and stacked them neatly on a pile in front of him.

'Here they are. They may not be any good.'

'They may not,' he agreed imperturbably. 'We'll leave that judgement to Granville. But if you don't want me to read them first, put them in a sealed envelope. We writers are incurably nosy about one another's work.'

This time her hesitation was perceptibly longer, for somehow the challenge was harder. Granville Stark barely knew her, his opinion would be purely professional and impersonal. But letting Luke read her stories was different . . . was like undressing in front of him, baring a part of herself for his critical inspection.

Perhaps she secretly longed to do that, too, but could not...dared not, for fear of where it might lead her. So she left the typewritten papers unsealed instead.

'Suit yourself,' she said with a shrug.

As if he ever did anything else!

# CHAPTER SEVEN

AMBER missed him when he wasn't there, and that, she knew, was not good. They rarely met without him challenging, disturbing or offending her in some way, but even their arguments added a zest to her life which was lacking during those few days he was away from Westbury. Alarmed, she realised how very quickly he could become necessary to her, like a drug which was dangerous but sweetly addictive, and she wished the term would pass more quickly, taking the danger of addiction away, once and for all.

On Saturday morning, a slim envelope dropped on to the doormat as Amber and Kate were having breakfast. Amber picked it up, eyed it suspiciously, trying to ascertain in advance whether or not it contained a bill, then slit it open philosophically. The letter inside bore the heading 'Granville Stark— Literary Agent', and a little knot of excitement tightened inside her as she read on.

> Dear Mrs Kingsland,
> Having read your three short stories, I am pleased to advise you that I consider I would be able to place one immediately, and the other two after minimal revision. Your work shows considerable promise, and on the strength of that I would be happy to take you as a client, should this be your wish. I understand you have a novel in the process of being written,

and would be interested to see a partial. Do telephone me for a chat—or better still, come up to London so we can have lunch together and a fuller discussion.

Amber jumped to her feet, knocking over the teapot and swamping the table in liquid.

'I don't believe it;' she shouted in incredulous triumph. 'Someone wants to publish my stories!'

Kate retrieved her toast from the soggy mess.

'Does that mean you'll be a real writer and make pots of money, like that man who came here?' she asked, adding wistfully, 'Perhaps I'd be able to have my very own pony then.'

'Let's not run before we can walk, love,' Amber said warmly. But contrarily her own ambitions were racing, if not leaping, ahead. Granville Stark liked her work and was prepared to take her as a client. She had her very own agent! And someone would actually pay to print what she had written! It was a dream come true, so fantastic she could scarcely believe it.

After she had belatedly mopped up the table, Amber made a fresh pot of tea and sat for a while, simply savouring her triumph. It was only a beginning. To finish and have accepted a full-length novel was another matter altogether, but at last—at last—her foot was on the ladder, and this hurdle which had loomed so large over the years had, in the end, been surmounted so easily.

Thanks to Luke Tremayne, she reminded herself soberly. She had been scribbling privately for years, and might have gone on that way for many more, never finding the nerve to take it any further, had he not provoked and challenged her into doing so.

And he had provided the contact, too. Amber did not doubt the old adage that in this world, it was *whom* you knew, as much as what you knew, which counted. She might have sent her typescript unsolicited to Granville Stark or anyone else, but agents received so much uninvited 'bumf', he might not have been motivated to read it. He'd read hers because Luke had asked him to.

Another thought crowded in on the heels of that one. Luke must have read her stories first, since she had indicated that he could. So he must also have thought she had some ability. If he'd found them utter rubbish, she knew he'd have brought them back to her and told her bluntly not to waste her time.

Her face grew warm as she pondered this realisation. Whatever she felt about Luke, his dubious personal life and attitudes, she owed him her thanks for what he had done on her behalf, and she did not think it would do to wait until she saw him around the university and offered him a few cool words of gratitude. Always impulsive, Amber could not, this morning, put her overflowing emotions on ice that long.

Depositing Kate at the stables where she helped with the tinies on Saturday mornings, Amber stayed just long enough to tell Lucy her wonderful news and bask in her congratulations. Then she drove into Westbury, did her usual weekly belt around the supermarket, loaded her groceries into the boot, and drove out to the river house.

Professor Doyle had said that Luke intended to be back for the weekend, and so he was, for his Jaguar was parked outside. So was a svelte little MGB she did not know, and Amber paused, checked in her headlong rush, and sat indecisively in her Mini with the engine still running. Luke had a guests—didn't he always, she thought ruefully, whenever she most wanted to see him? But this time she was forewarned, and would not go barging tactlessly in. Amber pushed the gear into reverse.

And then the door opened and Paula came out. The distance of the drive separated them, but Amber knew that the other woman had recognised her from their brief meeting at the party. She was also aware of something else—a guarded but very real hostility, advancing upon her wave by wave.

Having been spotted, she could hardly turn the car and scuttle away. It would have looked silly, and would also have been very difficult to explain. She switched off the engine and got out, rather sheepishly clutching Granville Stark's letter in her hand.

'Hello,' Paula said coolly, in the voice of one who always takes command of situations. 'I saw you at the party last week, didn't I?'

'Yes—I work at the university,' Amber said, trying not to be cowed by Paula's superior manner. 'I hope I'm not intruding. I just wanted a quick word with Luke.'

Paula looked as if she would have liked to refuse this request. Disdain and disapproval oozed from every pore of her—who was this inelegant female in the elderly Mini, to interrupt her Saturday *à deux* with her lover? But this was *Luke's* home, if only temporarily, and she was not quite in the position of châtelaine. Her lips tightened visibly, and Amber would have been glad to retreat if she could have done so with a measure of aplomb. The last thing she'd wanted was to bump into the percipient Mrs Grant again. Why couldn't common sense have told her that these two would be spending time here together whenever they could? Luke hadn't chosen this house simply to call her bluff, he had picked it for its suitability as a clandestine meeting place, and she, puzzling over his motives, had overlooked the most obvious!

But it was too late to make a run for it now, for here was Luke, in faded cords and a T-shirt which suggested he had been doing a bit of handiwork round the house, rather than entertaining his mistress! A benign, boyishly pleased smile spread across his face at the sight of Amber.

'You've had a letter from Granville,' he said, 'haven't you?'

'Yes, I have, and I just wanted to say thank you for your advice and help, which were both invaluable,' she said quickly.

'Go on with you!' He feigned embarrassment. 'I only put the stuff in front of his nose. *You* wrote it, it's good, and speaks for itself. I gather you've got yourself an agent now?'

Amber nodded. She knew she was grinning like a Cheshire cat, but even Paula's frosty presence could not completely dampen her pleasure, or her joy that he seemed to share it.

'Been pulling strings again, Luke?' Paula asked coolly.

And that sliced the bright, shining cake in half for her, making it sound as if Luke had a habit of encouraging new writers, and this was not something special he had done for her alone. But why should he have?

His voice was even as he said, 'Not really, I was only the go-between.' Turning to Amber, he said, 'Excuse us, we have to go out soon...I'm very glad for you, of course. Granville is a first-class agent, and you'll be in safe hands.'

Amber managed to half stumble back into her car, made a mess of a reverse turn that would have shamed a learner, and set off down the road faster than she should have done. She felt dismissed, discarded. Luke wasn't really all that interested in her meagre success. She had been mistaken to imagine that he was. Having set the wheels in motion for her, he did not want to be bothered with her concerns any further. Paula was here, and he had more important things to do.

Very well. If that was the way he wanted it—and plainly it was—she would not trouble him any more. Amber eased her foot off the accelerator pedal, bit her lip, and deliberately refused to wonder why hurt tears were stinging behind her eyes.

The professor was perfectly happy to allow Amber a day off work so that she could go and talk to her prospective agent.

'I'm very pleased for you, naturally,' he said. 'I only hope this new career doesn't mean we shall be losing your services.'

'I shouldn't think so,' she reassured him quickly, anxious to dispel any suspicion that she might be thinking of leaving. She couldn't afford to lose her job. 'Selling a few stories isn't going to make me a tax exile, and I really don't know yet whether I can properly make it as a writer.'

All the same, she could not deny her growing excitement as, wearing her best suit and with her hair done up as elegantly as possible, she dropped Kate off and caught the train to London.

Granville Stark could not have been kinder to her, or more encouraging. A well-known magazine had offered what seemed like a princely sum to Amber for one of her stories, and he quickly suggested how she could make the other two marketable.

'Some of these ideas are Luke's, I have to confess,' he smiled, over lunch in a smart French restaurant. 'As he says, this one is fine, except that you've started your narrative at the wrong point, and missed the opportunity to grab your reader by the throat. He, of course, is a master of the expert lead-in. If you don't grab a newspaper reader with your opening paragraph, you've lost him.'

Amber toyed with her *coquilles St-Jacques*. She both did and did not want to bring Luke into the conversation.

'I'll bear that in mind,' she said. 'Mr Stark—please be honest with me. Do you really think I've got what it takes?'

'If I'm going to represent you, you'd better start calling me Granville,' he said. 'My dear, if I didn't think you had potential, I wouldn't be here now, buying you an expensive lunch. Remember, I only earn if you do! Having said that—it's always a gamble. Now—what about this unfinished novel of yours? Do you feel like letting me see it?'

'I'd prefer to hold on to it a while longer, tidy it up a little—if it's all the same to you,' she said diffidently.

'You're the client.' He poured more wine into her glass. 'I'm simply here to give you advice, which you

may disregard if you wish.' He laughed. 'My per-
centage is just the same if you do.'

They retired to the bar-lounge for coffee, and while
they were drinking it a small party of people came in
and began ordering aperitifs at the bar. Amber had
her back to them, but that didn't prevent her from
recognising Paula's cool, authoritative voice and,
twisting her head slightly, she affirmed that she was
right.

'There's Mrs Grant,' she said, and Granville ac-
knowledged Paula with a brief salute.

'So it is—this is a popular rendezvous for literary
people,' he told her. 'Will you excuse me for a few
minutes? One of those chaps with her is someone I've
been wanting to have a word with for some time.'

Alone, Amber poured herself more coffee, and deliberately did not look round. She did not want to
catch Paula's eye. Luke's lady did not like her, that
was obvious, and to be honest, Amber admitted, the
feeling was wholly mutual!

'May I join you for a moment?'

Amber's surprise shaded into wariness. Paula's
voice was cool, but not unfriendly. Since she could
not decently refuse, she nodded, and with a swish of
crêpe de Chine the other woman sat beside her on the
velvet banquette.

'I wanted to congratulate you on making your first
break into this cut-throat business,' she said, with a
languid smile which did not quite reach her eyes,
Amber noted. 'You must have thought me rather rude
the other day, but the truth is, your arrival interrupted a rather serious conversation Luke and I were
having. You couldn't have known that, I realise.'

Amber was not sure why, but she did not at all trust this display of magnanimity. Still, she made an attempt to meet it half-way.

'I'm afraid I acted on impulse—it's a habit of mine,' she said. 'I just didn't think. Thank you, anyway. It's only a beginning, but it means a lot to me.'

'We all have to start somewhere,' Paula agreed condescendingly. 'You *do* seem to make a habit of bursting in on Luke at inopportune moments, don't you?'

Amber froze. The words were spoken lightly, but a threat, or a warning...or both...were somehow implied. She said, 'I beg your pardon?'

Paula said levelly, 'I knew I'd met you before, somewhere, and it's been puzzling me no end. It just came to me now. In the Dordogne, years ago. Surely you remember?'

Anmber thought, this is crazy. She knows I remember, and she probably worked out long before today where it was she had met me, although it doesn't sound as though she has said anything about it to Luke. She was suspicious, then, of my association with him, and it almost sounds as though she's still suspicious now. Warning me off before it gets to the stage where she has to turn a blind eye? She needn't worry!

'It *was* a long time ago,' she replied carefully, 'as you said.'

Paula sat back and eyed Amber reflectively.

'You may think you know Luke,' she said. 'A lot of people think that...a lot of women, particularly,' she emphasised. 'But they don't...not in the way that I do. We go back a long time.'

'You're mistaken,' Amber heard herself say, listening to her own frozen voice as if from a great distance. 'I hardly know him at all, Mrs Grant.'

Paula's slim shoulders rose and fell, she gave a sigh of resignation which Amber knew was an affectation. This woman had something to tell her, something she fully intended saying, and had not been reluctantly forced into divulging.

'You may as well know this,' she said. 'It will be common knowledge soon enough. I won't be Mrs Grant for much longer. Malcolm and I are getting a divorce.'

'I'm sorry,' Amber replied briefly. It seemed the safest comment to make, and she found herself wanting quite badly *not* to go into the deeper implications behind the statement. But Paula was equally determined that she should.

'It's strange about Luke and I,' she said. 'One of us is always tied up when the other is free. Or between relationships and in no state to make a commitment. He shouldn't have married Gemma. I shouldn't have married Malcolm. Maybe this time we'll get it right.'

There was nothing Amber could say in return for this information which, if she thought about it, she could probably have worked out for herself. Luke and Paula had been involved with each other for many years, and until now she had been unable to pin him down. Now she and her husband were splitting up, presumably on the grounds of her affair with Luke, and it looked as though she would get him at last. Even Luke Tremayne could not allow a woman to be dragged through the courts on account of him, and not stand by her afterwards, surely?

She was dimly aware of Granville's return, of his exchanging a few polite words with Paula, who then said, 'I'd better go, now. It looks as though our table is ready.'

Granville shook his head at her retreating back.

'That woman's a puzzle,' he said.

Not to me, she isn't, Amber thought wryly.

'She just told me she's getting a divorce,' she remarked.

He shot her a strange, surprised look.

'She told *you* that? I had heard the rumour, but I would hardly have expected her to be confiding it to passing acquaintances,' he replied. 'It's going to be a weird arrangement at Atkinson and Grant—unless she leaves, and I can't see her wanting to do that, or the company wanting her to. It would be a disaster for them if her authors went with her to another publisher—particularly Luke.'

'She and Luke have known one another for a long time, haven't they?' Amber could not resist querying, knowing she was fishing for information.

Granville only smiled, and poured more coffee.

'My dear, those are murky waters, and best left unstirred,' was all he would say.

Amber was unable to prevent a certain coolness in her manner towards Luke on her return to Westbury. She was still grateful to him for the part he had played in bringing about her collaboration with Granville Stark, but she could not cast from her mind the way he had virtually pushed her out when she had gone to say thank you.

Also—there was no point in denying it—she was upset by what she had learned about Paula and himself. If one believed what one read, the world was full of women eager to leap into bed with Luke Tremayne, but he, perversely, must have one who belonged to someone else, as if the fact that she had been his first gave him permanent rights. He must break up a marriage and hurt a man who was his friend.

When she probed more deeply into this vein of high moral outrage, she discovered that it wasn't only Luke's perfidy that distressed her. It was the knowledge that Luke was most probably going to marry Paula when her divorce became final. *Marry* her. Did that mean that really, in some part of his freebooting, free-loving soul, he loved this icily elegant woman as he had cared for no other? Had he loved her... without realising it himself... when he had married the mysterious Gemma, about whom Amber knew very little? And when he'd made love to *her*, by the pool, on that unforgettable day?

Amber tried to forget those illuminating moments when she and Luke had come close to understanding... she tried to forget the way she came alive when he entered a room... the way she still felt whenever he touched her. That was all it had ever been, she told herself scathingly, an overwhelming physical attraction which, in youthful ignorance, she had romanticised into love, and now recognised for what it was.

The man had immense talent, charm, undoubted courage; he could be thoughtful and considerate when it was least expected. He had many good qualities to set against the doubtful ones. But he was deeply, fatally flawed. It was best if she let him go his own way, as he would, without allowing it to concern her any more than it had to.

'So it all went well with Granville?' he asked her, and she nodded coolly.

'Very well, thank you.'

'That's all you're going to tell me?' he sighed with mock sadness. 'Ah, that's the way it is. Once they acheive fame and fortune, they don't want to know you any more!'

Amber knew this mood of facetious amusement, and it never failed to alert her guard.

'Don't be silly, Luke. There's nothing to tell that you don't already know, since you read the stories first and suggested the revisions... for which I'm grateful. Granville and I had lunch together. Oh... and we saw Paula in the restaurant.'

'Really? She didn't tell me that when I spoke to her on the phone,' he said. 'Did you talk to her?'

'Oh, yes, we had quite a chat. She told me about her divorce,' Amber said brightly. *That* will shut him up, she thought viciously.

Luke shook his head.

'Messy business,' he said, for all the world as if it did not concern himself. 'Poor Paula—that's the trouble with marriage. It comes with built-in obsolescence.'

At this, Amber was so disgusted she could only turn away, applying herself resolutely to her work. And after that day he appeared to take his cue from her. She saw him occasionally around the university, but he never came to the office without a specific reason. Now and then they were a part of the same lunchtime crowd eating sandwiches at the pub, but he paid her no particular attention.

With something of a shock, Amber realised that what she had prayed for was happening. The term was passing quickly, they were well into June, with only a couple of weeks to go, and it would appear she had got away with it. Luke Tremayne would go his way, none the wiser, and all they would have in common was the same literary agent—which did not necessarily mean they need meet again. Otherwise, her life would be as it was before. She wished she could feel happier about it.

The students had started to talk about finals and vacations, weighing up the pros and cons of holiday jobs—grape-picking versus skivvying in restaurant kitchens. The staff had their minds on fresh pastures, too.

'I'm going to do Tuscany,' Sorrel said loftily. 'Florence, Siena, Bologna—all the Renaissance cities and art treasures. Aren't you envious?'

'Hell, no!' Cal said cheerfully. 'My folks have a holiday home up in Maine. I'm gong to sail and fish and lie on the beach all summer.'

'Philistine!' Sorrel said distastefully.

'Aesthete!' he retorted, unperturbed. 'What are you going to do, Luke? Is the *Examiner* sending you off anywhere dangerous?'

'Probably, but I never know where until it happens,' he said. 'I'm going to work on my book; I've done very little since I've been at Westbury, and my publishers will be screaming.'

'Poor you,' Sorrel commiserated.

'It's not so bad as it sounds,' he said. 'I own a house in France, so I shall spend most of the summer working there. Then I can have the benefit of the sun and the food.' His eyes met Amber's only briefly, impersonally, then returned to the company at large as he said, 'Some years ago, I rented this dilapidated farmhouse in the Dordogne. I grew fond of it, so when I was in a financial position to do so, I bought it and restored it. I go out there whenever I get the chance—it's my bolt-hole.'

Amber could not finish her sandwich. Another thing he had not told her—that she had no reason to expect him to tell her. The place where she had once fallen in love with him was not just another patchwork piece of his many-coloured past. It was his home, the place he chose to return to whenever he could. The place where he took Paula, and would take her as his wife?

'Amber? You don't seem to be very hungry today,' Cal remarked.

She forced a smile.

'I have to get back. There are some students' assessments I have to finish typing today,' she excused herself. And retreated, somehow, without looking in Luke's direction.

There was always a fraught, hectic atmosphere around the university when finals were being sat. Even the students who were not in their final year had assessments and examinations, but all the same there was a sizeable gathering in the lecture-room to hear Luke Tremayne's talk on the life and work of modern Russian author, Alexander Solzhenitsyn, his last session with the students of Westbury.

Amber would have liked to sit in on this, if only for a few minutes. She was interested in what comparisons and analogies Luke would draw between what the man had written and the eventful course of his life. But she resisted her curious impulse for once, considering it more important that she kept herself out of Luke's way.

She did not know when exactly he was planning to leave Westbury, but it could not be too far in the future. He had no reason to prolong his stay once his lectures were finished and the assignments he had set were marked—he could pack his bags and vanish off to his house in France.

She closed her eyes briefly, trying to shut out the pain this image caused her—the sun on the old red roof-tiles, the long grass, the dusty drive.

'A book of verse...a jug of wine...and thou beside me, singing in the wilderness.' How short a song it had turned out to be, cut off almost before it had begun.

The final Saturday before the end of term arrived, and with it Amber's cheque for the accepted story, due to be published shortly. It had seemed a lot of money when Granville first named the amount, but it wasn't, of course. She still was not in a position to take Kate away on holiday, but they both needed new summer clothes, and the sales were on in Westbury. Perhaps she could indulge in a little spending without feeling too guilty about it.

As a consequence of this decision, she was late getting back from shopping to pick up Kate from the stables. Not that it would bother her—her daughter was always happiest around horses.

Parking the car, she saw Kate coming across the field mounted on Beauty, her favourite pony. She wasn't alone. Her companion was riding Scarlet, Lucy's liveliest and most temperamental mare, whom he seemed to have under perfect control. His polished leather boots shone in the sunlight, contrasting with a hacking jacket which, although of excellent quality, looked as if it had been in his possession for many years, and his bright hair gleamed with red glints as he tossed it carelessly back from his forehead.

Luke Tremayne! Riding with *her* daughter—his daughter! Amber swallowed, biting hard on the pang of emotion which gripped her at this sight. She allowed a fierce indignation to swamp it. He had no right—none at all! Getting out of the car, she slammed the door harder than she should have, in view of the vehicle's age, and strode across the paddock.

Kate reined in as she drew alongside, and waved cheerily to her mother, but Amber's approach made Scarlet skittish, and Luke expertly brought the prancing animal under control.

'We had a great ride,' Kate said happily, cheeks brilliant. 'Right across the fields, past the church and back! Luke wanted to take Scarlet out, so Lucy said I could go with him.'

'So I see,' Amber said. Kate looked so exultant and glowing with life, she hadn't the heart to spoil her child's pleasure, although she was spilling over with questions. Why was Luke here, riding with Kate, and just what was he up to?

'I didn't know you rode,' she said tightly, condensing all her doubts and apprehensions into those few terse words.

'I used to, quite a lot, when I was younger and had more time,' he said, sliding easily from Scarlet's back and patting her nose affectionately. 'I learned when I was about Kate's age. So when I felt in need of a little exercise, I remembered your daughter went to a riding stable close by here.'

He smiled at Kate as she dismounted, and she returned his smile in an open, friendly manner. It was not difficult to see that she had enjoyed his company, and Amber was suddenly very glad that he would soon be leaving.

'Come on, young lady, let's get these horses in,' he said.

'We'll be in the tack-room, Mum. See you in a few minutes,' Kate responded jauntily.

Amber watched them walk off. Why had she never before noticed the set of Kate's determined shoulders, so much like that of the man by her side? She turned away, not wanting to find any further resemblance, and stood leaning against the fence, tapping her foot impatiently. She was all at once desperately anxious to get away, and wished she could simply have gathered up her child and fled. Unfortunately, Kate was not a parcel to be picked up and despatched out of harm's way, but a spirited girl with a mind of her own, and decidedly independent ways!

Lucy came over to stand by her side.

'Time for me to take a breather, now the tots have finished their lesson,' she said. She smiled knowingly. 'Your friend Luke is quite a charmer, isn't he? I could go for him in a big way!'

'He's not my friend,' Amber stated firmly. 'I'm not so sure that I approve of Kate riding with him, come to that.'

'Why not?' Lucy looked genuinely puzzled. 'They seemed to be getting on like a house on fire.'

'He has an unsavoury reputation,' Amber said, unable to think of any other objection she could safely make to Lucy.

'Yes—but with females considerably older than Kate!' Lucy said, shocked. 'He wouldn't harm her, and you know it! Since you weren't here, I used my own judgement, and to be honest, I still can't see why they shouldn't ride together. However, you're her mother. I won't let it happen again, if you disapprove.'

Amber had not meant to hurt her friend, but she saw that she had, by appearing to doubt her instincts.

'I'm sorry, Lucy. I guess I'm becoming a mite over-protective,' she said. 'Don't worry about it—Luke won't be here for much longer.

It seemed an age before her daughter and Luke Tremayne strolled over from the tack-room, still deep in conversation. Amber wondered forebodingly what they were finding to talk about.

'I'm starving!' Kate announced characteristically, as soon as she came within earshot of Amber. 'Are we going to have lunch, now?'

'As soon as we get home,' Amber said, holding the door open for Kate to scramble into the back seat of the Mini.

'Good.' Kate bounced up and down energetically. 'I said Luke could come back and eat lunch with us. That's OK, isn't it?'

Amber was so taken aback, she could only mutter lamely, 'Well, Kate, I'm sure that Luke will be very busy, and——' She glanced up at him, expecting him to take her cue, but he seemed untroubled by her obvious unwillingness.

'On the contrary, I don't have a thing to do,' he assured her blithely. 'I'd be delighted—if that's all right by you.'

It wasn't, and he must have been aware from her face and her manner that it wasn't, but he smiled expectantly, as if perfectly sure of a welcome, and Kate grinned cheerfully, too. It was difficult for Amber to find an instantly acceptable excuse that was also suitably polite.

'Oh . . . that's fine,' she said hurriedly, 'so long as you don't mind pot luck. It won't be anything special.'

'You go and put the pot on,' he told her, still smiling. 'I'll follow in my car.'

Driving home, Amber could not hold in her annoyance and unease any longer.

'That wasn't very thoughtful of you, love,' she reproached her daughter. 'Haven't I always told you to ask me first, before you invite someone? After all, how do you know I have anything suitable to give guests?'

'But you've just been to the supermarket this morning,' Kate objected reasonably. 'I thought it would be OK to ask Luke. I like him, Mum. We had a really good talk.'

'What about?' Amber asked nervously. The nearer she got to home, the louder the warning drums were beating in her brain, urging her not to let him invade her sanctuary, and worm his way into her daughter's affections.

'Horses, mostly. He told me about this friend he stayed with in California, who breeds palominos. It was really interesting. And he talks to you as if you're a real person, not just a kid.'

She's lacked the presence of a man in her life, Amber thought as she parked the car. It's no wonder she finds Luke fascinating, intriguing—and fun! It would be all too easy for her to start looking to him as a father-figure, especially as he had the automatic advantage of being knowledgeable about horses—

blast him! But she couldn't allow that. Hopefully, he would be gone within the week, and she'd find some excuse to keep the lunch mercifully short—say she had to take Kate shopping. Only she knew that she had spent most of her unexpected windfall that morning!

It was strange to be beating eggs and grating cheese to make omelettes for Kate and Luke, who were engaged in a spirited discussion of the merits of various breeds of horse. Like playing at happy families, Amber thought, her stomach churning crazily, but I'm the only one who knows . . .

She slid the first omelette on to the plate, put it in the oven to keep warm. This was ridiculous. They were not in any way a family, and sitting round a table together would not make them so. Kate was *her* child, she had brought her up, nursed her through her illnesses, loved her, wept with her.

The second omelette followed the first, and Amber started on the last one.

' . . . but Morgans are *very* special horses, don't you think so?' Kate was demanding eagerly.

Without meaning to, Amber found her eyes engaged with Luke's.

'Your daughter is a mine of information,' he said wryly. 'I never met a nine-year-old girl with quite so much specialist knowledge!'

*'Nine?'* Kate squeaked indignantly. 'I'm ten! Do I look as if I'm only nine?'

Amber, dishing up the last of the omelettes, seemed to see herself moving in slow motion, every breath taking an infinity to draw, every action taking aeons to complete. She looked at her daughter, saw the sprinkle of freckles across the bridge of her nose, the jut of her assertive jaw, and wondered faintly how she could have failed to see what now, looking at them together, was shrieking at her.

'I do apologise,' Luke said. 'It was your mother who told me you were nine, so I assumed she would know.'

'Mum!' Kate cried reproachfully. 'You know I had a birthday at Easter!'

She couldn't speak. All the passages that carried air to her lungs were blocked. Time slowed down again, stretching out every second that passed until she was able to say lightly, 'Silly me. So you did. I must have forgotten. Here—eat your omelettes before they get cold.'

She ate hers, every bite, although it was forced work, and at any moment she expected her stomach to revolt. She talked, too—insignificant, inconsequential chat, which did not quite succeed in fending off the accusing spotlight of Luke's eyes, trained on her from across the table.

She had gambled and lost, and did not dare to think what the price of that defeat was going to be.

# CHAPTER EIGHT

LUKE waited with implacable patience until Kate tired of inactivity, took her fishing-net, and went off down to the nearby stream. But the waiting had not cooled his anger, only added fuel to it. Amber had never seen him like this, so coldly, unforgivingly furious, eyes blazing icily in a face that was hard as cast bronze.

'Are you going to tell me the truth?' he demanded, 'Or do I have to force it out of you?'

Amber was alarmed to the point of fear, but she held her ground.

'What *is* all this nonsense? I'm afraid I don't understand you,' she bluffed.

'You understand me perfectly. No mother forgets her own child's birthday, or reckons it out by a year!' he declared scornfully. 'You lied to me deliberately. Kate is ten. If her birthday was at Easter, and you and I were together in July... I know it was, because I rented the farmhouse for the whole of that month... then by my arithmetic, that makes her my child.'

'Kate is Lawrence's daughter!' Amber lied desperately, knowing that the ground beneath her feet was as insubstantial as swampland. 'How can you say she isn't? I knew him before I knew you!'

'Not in the biblical sense of the word,' he reminded her drily. 'You were a virgin on that day, Amber. I was the first, and don't deny it. No wonder you wanted to keep quiet about our past liaison. People

141

would have started to ask questions, wouldn't they, and put two and two together? It would have come to my ears, and I'd have found out that you'd kept from me for ten years the fact that I had a daughter!'

He paced the room disgustedly, and Amber found she was hugging herself tightly, holding in her wretchedness. 'And I colluded with you—swallowed your phoney reasons!' he exclaimed contemptuously. 'The day you came to thank me when Granville liked your work, I even sent you away quickly, in case Paula recognised you and started talking about your past! Amber, you make me sick! How could you do it? Did it never occur to you that as a father I had some rights?'

Amber stopped pretending at that. Anger charged her misery, sending a welcome burst of adrenalin along her veins. Hostility blazed at him from her slanting green eyes.

'What rights?' she demanded scornfully. 'You plunder a woman's body, then cast her aside when you've done with it, and think that gives you *rights*? You're sick all right, Luke, but it isn't I who made you so!'

'I did not "cast you aside" as you so slanderously put it,' he said coldly. 'You should choose your words more carefully Amber. So far as I'm concerned, you're still wearing L-plates! I offered you whatever help you might need, in the eventuality of your being pregnant.'

'Oh, yes—like a quick abortion, or a cheque in the post every month!' Amber retorted, with swift and immediate contempt. 'Can you wonder I preferred someone who really cared for me, and was prepared to be a father to Kate?'

She thought he winced, but only very slightly.

'No,' he said. 'I wasn't ready to be married to anyone at that time, and I'd have made a pretty disastrous husband. What I'm saying is, you were wrong to keep it from me. Like it or not, I am Kate's father.'

Moving very quickly, with the speed of one whose life had often depended on his ability to do just that, he grasped her wrist, his fingers squeezing so hard that she thought the delicate bones would be crushed.

'I *am* her father. Aren't I?' he demanded. She turned her head away, refusing to answer, and the fingers tightened implacably, pulling her towards him. It hurt—excruciatingly, but she bit her lip and forbore to cry out. 'Aren't I?'

With equal suddenness, he let her go, so that she staggered back, bracing herself against the pine dresser.

'You're incapable of the truth,' he said brutally.

Amber stared at him. Her wrist was throbbing, and tomorrow, she knew, there would be a bruise empurpling the pale, creamy skin. But that counted little compared to the pain burning within her, a wrenching anguish, rage, shame and regret, so intermingled that she could not disentangle their separate strands.

What forced the admission that his harsh treatment had been unable to wring from her was the sight of that pain mirrored in the agonised blue eyes.

'Yes,' she said defeatedly. 'She's yours. If it makes you feel any better to hear me admit it. But what difference can it possibly make now, Luke? It's too late.'

'You think it makes no difference?' His voice was coldly incredulous. 'You rob me of ten years of my daughter's life, and now you want me to go away and pretend I don't know about her, and she has nothing to do with me? Is that what you expect of me?'

Amber's thoughts sped back to those difficult days when she had found she was pregnant; then, like the reel of a film running at great speed, relived the years with Lawrence—the arguments, the suspicion, the jealousy. *She* was the one who had endured all that, for Kate's sake, and if that did not make the child wholly hers, then she did not know what did.

'Yes!' she flung back at him defiantly. 'That's precisely what I expect. Kate thinks of Lawrence as her father. She loved him, and he was good to her. I don't want her to learn otherwise.'

His eyes had narrowed to angry, calculating slits, from which pinpoints of harsh brilliance lasered into her.

'So that's the attitude you're going to take, is it?' he challenged. 'You think you can cut me out of Kate's future, too? You're a fool, Amber, and if you really cared for your daughter, you'd realise that there is a lot I could do for her.'

She glanced defensively around at her second-hand furniture in its shabbily comfortable setting.

'No, thank you. I didn't want your money then, and I don't want it now. We can manage. Just go away and leave us in peace, Luke. That's all I ask of you.'

He was silent for a few moments, and then he sighed heavily.

'You don't leave me an awful lot of room for manoeuvre, do you?' he asked. 'There's a hard way and an easy way. We could reach an amicable agreement...or I could get my lawyers on it and fight you through the courts for, at the very least, the right of access to my own child.'

His words almost deprived her of breath.

'You wouldn't!' she choked thickly, but one glance into the still hard blue eyes told her that he wasn't bluffing. 'You could never prove it!' she countered fiercely. 'I'd fight you—I'd swear under oath, if I had to, that Kate was Lawrence's, before I'd let you take her from me!'

'I don't doubt that you'd perjure yourself, Amber,' he said cuttingly. 'But cases like this cost money, which wouldn't be my problem. I have it, and I'd use it. You think I couldn't provide proof? Who knows... there are blood tests, and so forth. Certainly, I could stir up enough doubt.'

Amber stared at him numbly. She had been married to Lawrence at the time of Kate's birth, and he was registered as the father. Was that enough, when the child had clearly been conceived out of wedlock? She did not know enough about the law to be sure, but one thing she did know. If Luke went ahead and carried out his threat, there was no power great enough to keep this thing under wraps. Everyone would know, the scandal would rock Westbury, shatter their lives, hers and Kate's... poor, poor Kate, she thought wretchedly, how could she cope with the storm of publicity which would break over her innocent head?

'Are you thinking what I'm thinking?' Luke asked softly. 'A certain section of the Press will have a field day with this... won't they?'

She hated him at that moment with more venom than she had ever known was in her nature. He had beaten her and she knew it, for she would not subject Kate to such horrors as he predicted. From here on, he called all the shots, and there was precious little she could do to stop him, with that threat hanging over her.

'What's the easy way?' she whispered, sickened by her own capitulation, but seeing no way out of it.

His eyes teased her arrogantly, daring her to defy him again, all the while knowing that he had tied her hands.

'Singing a different tune now, are we?' he asked tauntingly. 'Right then, let's see. As I understand it, your main consideration, apart from the obvious one of keeping custody of Kate, is to prevent her from learning about her parentage in a blaze of publicity.'

'I'd rather she didn't learn at all.' Even in defeat, she could not resist this final barb. 'I'm fussy about the kind of man *my* child calls father, and I don't want her embroiled in the tangles of your love-life.'

Surprisingly, he laughed.

'Oh, Amber! My wild oats are well and truly sown. I'm a staid character now, didn't you know?'

She supposed he was referring to his eventual marriage to Paula, and forbore to remind him that there was a messy divorce to go through first.

Then, even more surprisingly, he said, 'All right, I agree to condition one. Kate doesn't learn that I'm her father unless and until you choose to tell her. Fair enough?'

It was—far more than she had ever hoped he would concede, for, if he could not acknowledge paternity and claim Kate as his daughter, what was in it for him? She gazed up at him, puzzled, suspicious, at a loss to understand why, having been so harsh and threatening, he was now giving her back the trump card.

'But I'll never do that,' she thought it only fair to tell him.

'Never is a long time, Amber.' He raised a hand and gently pushed back the mahogany tendrils clinging to her cheek. His fingers grazed her skin and she flinched, because even now he could arouse desire in her.

'What do you want, Luke? I don't understand,' she said abruptly, moving away from him.

He did not pursue her.

'I'm not going to ride off into the sunset and disappear,' he stated firmly. 'What I want is a watching brief. The right to be kept informed, to be called on if needed. I don't think that's asking too much.'

Amber was feeling so faint with relief that she almost nodded agreement, for it seemed he was giving her most of what she already had. So maybe she would have to see him occasionally, or discreetly arrange to let him see Kate. She would have to send progress reports, give an account of what Kate was doing. Call on him for help? She glossed over that proviso, it would never happen. Otherwise, she and Kate would continue to live as they always had.

'Is that all?' she asked, incredulously, and he smiled.

'You see? Not so terrible, is it? I'd like to contribute to my daughter's upkeep, of course.'

'No!' Her response was immediate. 'Not money! I won't accept it, Luke.'

'Who's dictating the terms here?' he demanded, with just a glimmer of amusement. 'I could stop a stray bullet at any time, Amber, and you've no jurisdiction over whether I leave my ill-gotten gains to Kate or the Battersea Dogs' Home.'

'Don't!' The plea was wrung from her against her will, but she could not calmly accept the possibility of violent death that he had so dispassionately described. The worst part was that she knew he was not exaggerating.

'I've led a charmed life so far, but you know it's true,' he said quietly. 'So we have to thrash this out now, in case the *Examiner* sends me somewhere tomorrow and I don't come back. But let's be optimistic and assume I haven't used up all my nine lives. I'll start a trust fund for Kate, for when she's eighteen. You can always invent a convenient long-lost uncle in Australia.'

Amber had begun to feel decidedly strange. The shock of his discovery, the hard words they had exchanged, and now this grim discussion of the realities of life and death, all told on her, and suddenly she was aware of a sagging sensation at her knees, a draining of the blood from her face.

He saw it, too, and before she realised it she was propped up in a chair, his arm round her. It was incomprehensible . . . he was the author of her troubles, and yet she wanted to lean against him, to abdicate her responsibility for her life and herself, and give them into his hands. It must be reaction, nothing more, she decided.

'You all right?' he asked.

'I'll live,' she said shortly.

'I'm relieved to hear it. But I think we'd better have a cup of strong tea. Nothing like it in a crisis,' he observed cheerfully. 'No—don't move. I'll make it. I make damn good tea.'

Strong was certainly the word, Amber thought, as she sipped the dark, murky liquid.

'Ugh—there must be half a pound of tea leaves in there,' she complained. 'It's ghastly!'

He grinned.

'Get it down you. It will put hairs on your chest,' he said, and then, with an oblique glance at that part of her anatomy, 'On second thoughts—perhaps not. Oh, by the way——' His light tone, carrying on from the jocular remarks preceding it, took her completely unawares, a sudden, surprise attack for which she was totally unprepared. 'There's one more condition to our deal. I'm going to my place in France to work on my book, and I want you to come out with me and type up the manuscript as I go along.'

She was bolt upright again now, the weakness all gone.

'Me? But how long for?' she demanded in a panic.

'Oh...for what's left of the summer, depending on how fast I write, and how well you type.' He smiled, enjoying her discomfiture. 'You've time to get your passports arranged.'

Spend the whole summer with him in that farmhouse in the Perigord? Her whole being cried out against the prospect.

'I'd rather not go, Luke,' she said quietly. 'Any agency will supply you with a typist who'd jump at the chance.'

'I'm sure,' he agreed. 'But I want you. I think it would be...appropriate for you to go back to where it all started, to where you conceived our daughter. The one you tried to keep from me. Look on it as a penance, if you like. Or just as an extra job—I'll pay you, of course.' His mouth hardened. 'Look on it how you like, but you're going, or the deal's off. It's not negotiable.'

Amber was quiet as she drank the rest of her tea, no longer noticing how it tasted. She had known there would be a catch, and this was it. Did he think he was teaching her some kind of lesson, forcing her to go back and confront her own past?

When Tiger, their cat, had been small, and had made puddles in corners, Lucy had advised her to rub his nose in it as a punishment and deterrent, and she supposed what he had in mind worked on the same principle. As if she would ever behave so stupidly again, she thought disgustedly.

'Will . . . will Paula be there?' she asked.

'Probably, for part of the time. Granville and Clarissa might come out, too,' he said blandly. 'Don't worry, we shan't be sequestered there alone all summer. My intentions aren't lecherous.'

'I never for one minute thought they were,' Amber said haughtily. You'll have Paula for that purpose, won't you? she felt like adding. She would have to go through it all again, watching them together, knowing that he belonged to someone else. She was terribly afraid that it was going to hurt.

But why should it? She had been in love with him before, and that was what had made it so painful. She'd been young and romantic and innocent. Now she was none of those things. She was a mature woman who'd been married, borne a child, lost a husband. She'd changed too much for such ancient scars to be re-opened.

Maybe Luke had awoken in her the dormant, un-assuaged sexuality that he had been the first . . . the only one . . . to stir. And, despise herself for it as she did, sometimes she awoke in the night full of an aching desire to be in his arms.

'But I *don't* love him,' she told herself firmly as she watched him climb into the Jaguar and drive away.

'He's Paula's, and she can have him! Any woman foolish enough to love him needs her head examining!'

Once bitten, twice shy. She could never be that foolish a second time.

It was Kate herself who put the idea in her head, quite unwittingly, showing Amber a way she could go along with Luke, while at the same time defying him.

'Do I have to go?' she asked, when Amber first tentatively mentioned the trip to France. 'I mean, I like Luke a lot, and it would be fun, but I'm riding in two gymkhanas this summer, and I'd have to miss them, wouldn't I?'

A thoughtful gleam crept into Amber's eyes as she regarded her child. She had no doubt that Luke expected her to bring Kate along so he could take this surreptitious opportunity to get to know her better. He thought he had got her exactly where he wanted her, and she was in a position to refuse him nothing, but she could still outwit him and preserve a measure of independent action.

'I reckon you could stay with Lucy, if she'll have you,' she said, knowing that Lucy, who had been like a second mother to Kate for so many years, was unlikely to quibble at the prospect. 'I'm going to be working most of the time, anyhow, which would be a bit of a bore for you, and it would be a shame for you to miss the gymkhanas.'

Kate grinned broadly, then suddenly and uncharacteristically, for she was not given to displays of emotion, flung her arms round Amber's neck.

'I'll miss you,' she declared.

'Hey—I haven't gone yet!' Amber laughed, hiding her natural apprehension at being separated from her daughter for the first time. 'I'll miss you too, but we can write and telephone. And it isn't that far away.'

She was glad now of the new summer clothes she'd invested in. Her morale was going to need every last bit of help it could get to cope with a summer spent under the same roof as Luke, and looking shabby was the last thing she needed—even if she couldn't compete with Paula and her designer wardrobe. Amber washed, ironed and packed carefully everything she thought she would need.

'I hear you're going to France with Luke,' Sorrel said interestedly. 'That should be quite an experience.'

Amber kept her expression deliberately blank.

'He needs a typist—and I, as always, need money,' she replied. 'It isn't a holiday.'

'It won't be all work,' Luke said, picking up the last few words as he joined them. 'You'll have some time for leisure and sightseeing.'

'I'd sooner get the work done more quickly, so I can get home,' Amber said pointedly. 'When do you leave for Tuscany, Sorrel?'

'Oh, haven't you heard?' Cal grinned. 'Sorrel has decided to give Italy a miss. She's coming to Maine with me.'

Amber was surprised and showed it.

'Well . . . *that* will be quite an experience,' she said with a little smile, and astonishingly the svelte, assured young woman blushed faintly.

'Does that amaze you so much?' Luke asked, when the other two had gone.

'You don't know them as well as I do,' she retorted. 'They've been at each other's throats for three years, to my knowledge.'

'And *you* don't know a great deal about male/ female relationships,' he remarked lightly. 'They're crazy about each other, only it's taken them a while to realise it, and they're not quite at the point where they're ready to admit it. It should be a revealing summer for them.'

'Gosh! I'll just have to write to Uncle Luke's agony column when I need a bit of advice,' Amber said, opening her eyes ingenuously wide. 'I should have realised experience has made you an expert!'

He laughed, but something in his voice warned her not to push her luck too far. In a matter of days they would be in France together, where there would be no easy escape from him, and if he chose to make it unpleasant for her he could do so.

'To get back to our own trip, I've booked us an overnight crossing to Le Havre, so we should be able to drive down in one day without difficulty,' he said. 'It might mean a late arrival, but Kate can always sleep in the car if she gets tired.'

Amber had been waiting to savour this small moment of triumph.

'Kate won't be coming with me,' she announced casually. 'I'm leaving her with Lucy. She's riding in two gymkhanas, and I'm sure you wouldn't want her to miss them. Besides, you don't need *her* to type your manuscript.'

He didn't reply immediately, but his eyes gave her a long and thorough. examination, in which she thought she discerned a faint glimmer of respect.

'Very clever, Amber,' he said softly. 'If you want to make an adversary of me, you can. Your choice, not mine.'

She returned his stare calmly.

'You may feel it's your right to get to know Kate. I don't want her exposed too much to your life-style,' she replied levelly.

'Um...this...er...life-style of mine. Are you confident it's safe to expose yourself to it?' he asked with malicious humour.

'You didn't give me any choice,' she reminded him triumphantly. He shrugged, smiled, and allowed her to have the last word, but she derived small comfort from this meagre victory. Because she was far from confident, and he must surely know it.

As Luke had predicted, they arrived at Tarsac very late, after darkness had fallen. The journey was nothing like the gentle meander through France she had taken with Uncle Selwyn. Luke was not pottering, but in a hurry to reach his destination, and he drove at a fast, steady pace along the excellent network of long, straight, unexpectedly empty roads which made driving in France a revelation to British motorists.

Now and then he encouraged Amber to take the wheel while he had a rest. She quailed at first, never having driven such a powerful, expensive motor before, but quickly found it an enjoyable experience, and she had to admit it was a pleasant novelty to be driving a vehicle other motorists viewed with respect and admiration.

They stopped just after Tours for lunch in a riverside village—not the long, leisurely *déjeuner* the other diners were enjoying, but a brief, alcohol-free break, and then set off again. Beyond Limoges, she was aware of a gradual transition to the lands of the south, a softness in the air, rolling, hilly countryside, the ochre-red tiles replacing grey slate on the roofs. Dusk had fallen as they negotiated the wooded gorges through which the road wound, and it was quite dark as they drove through Les Eyzies, the 'capital' of pre-history, where many of the famous caves were situated.

By night, it was difficult for Amber to recognise the winding country road she'd ridden along on her bike, but the sluggish swishing of the Vezere river which for part of the way ran alongside it brought back a rush of memories. And then there was Tarsac. A small, dusty square where old men would play *boules* in the cool of the evening, a few iron benches, trees to provide shade. A little church, one general purpose *épicerie*, a scattering of houses ... and the Auberge du Pont, looking remarkably as it had looked before.

'It hasn't changed,' Luke said quietly. 'That's why I like it. The French village in microcosm.'

Amber was biting her lip hard and clenching her hands, hidden in her lap, as he drove out along the road towards the farmhouse. The place was thick with memories she did not want to have to re-examine— old hurts, old shame, and, yes, old delights, too. If she could close her eyes until morning, she would at least be able to postpone her reacquaintance with them.

The drive was smoother than she remembered it, gravel gleaming whitely in the moonlight as the Jaguar swept towards the house.

'I had it levelled,' Luke remarked. 'Very pictur-esque, all those bumps, but bad for your car's sus-pension. People kept complaining and sending me their garage bills. Here we are, then.'

Amber got out slowly, looking around her. It was the same house, of course, but even by moonlight she could see the amount of loving, careful restoration which had been done. The roof had been re-tiled, but in the original dull terracotta local tiles, there were new wooden shutters at all the windows, and the terrace had been re-flagged, was free of weeds, and furnished with wrought-iron tables and chairs. The grass was mown, and there were roses and pelargoniums in stone urns. It both was, and was not, the place she remembered.

'Cost me a bomb,' he said cheerfully, fitting the key into the lock. 'But I've enjoyed every minute of the process, and I think the result is worth it.'

Inside there was the same stylishly comfortable mixture of old and new, dark French provincial furniture and softer, more modern upholstered settees and chairs, antique light fittings and a huge stone fireplace with logs already in place.

'I think we will have a fire,' he said, striking a match. 'It will probably be hot tomorrow, but the house has been empty for a while. Pop into the kitchen, Amber, and see what *madame*, who "does" for me, has left us. I told her we would be arriving tonight.'

She did as he told her, as if in a daze, still without having spoken a word since the car drew up outside. Along the corridor, past the cloakroom where she'd hidden and eavesdropped on his conversation with Paula—his lover, then and now, she reflected as she found the kitchen, which was well fitted out with dark oak units camouflaging every modern necessity.

In the fridge she found a mouthwatering selection of *charcuterie*, cooked meats and delicatessen, half a cooked chicken, salad in a bowl, and several huge wedges of cheese. There was a bottle of Muscadet, which she uncorked after a brief hesitation, then she hunted for coffee and spooned some into the machine. Plates, glasses, cutlery and a tray—she piled up the lot and carried it back to the room where she had left him.

'Well done,' he said, as if the provision of this bounty were all her own work, taking the tray from her and setting it on a low table in front of the now crackling fire. 'Tuck in—I'm ravenous, aren't you?'

Amber perched uneasily on the edge of a settee, but he squatted cross-legged on the floor.

'It's much better down here,' he said invitingly. 'Don't worry—after driving five hundred miles in a day, I haven't the energy left to molest you.'

She jumped to her feet, suddenly quivering with nerves. 'I'll see if the coffee's ready.'

In the kitchen she poured coffee with hands that trembled. She did not hear his footfalls on the corridor, but all at once knew he was behind her. His hands rested on her shoulders, and she felt his breath against her hair.

'You could at least try to relax,' he said quietly.

'I can't,' she whispered. 'How can I feel at ease when I know why you've brought me here? Not to type your wretched manuscript—any half-competent agency typist could do that—but to make me feel bad for keeping Kate's existence from you all these years.'

He turned her towards him, still keeping his hands firm and steady on her shoulders.

'And if that's true, it wouldn't be too high a payment to ask,' he said, his voice dangerously unemotional. 'A few weeks of feeling vaguely guilty, in

return for ten years of my daughter's life you stole—
yes, *stole* from me. Irreplaceable years you can never
give back. You wanted it both ways, Amber, didn't
you? The young man you were in love with, and the
child of our brief fling. And so you had it, for several
years. And even though you lost Lawrence, you're
still trading on your Romeo and Juliet marriage.
Everyone admires you, respects you, gallant Amber,
who loved and lost bringing up her dead husband's
child all alone! Until I came along, threatening to
upset the apple-cart, and you couldn't have that, could
you?'

The soft, ever so slightly sarcastic voice was quite
pitiless, and the irony of it all was that he did not
know she had never loved Lawrence, and that it was
the memory of him which had prevented her. The
version he'd heard was the version everyone else believed, which she had thought it wise never to con-
tradict. Wisest of all, now, to let him go on thinking
it.

'I'm tired, Luke,' she said woodenly. 'I can't take
any more—not tonight.

He dropped his hands abruptly, as if he, too, had
reached the end of some private tether.

' "Sufficient unto the day is the evil thereof," ' he
quoted wryly. 'You're right. Let us take ourselves off
to our separate beds—after I've shown you where
yours is. And you don't need to worry—I don't
sleepwalk.'

# CHAPTER NINE

AMBER woke to a sparkling morning with sunlight beating importunately at the wooden shutters of her bedroom window. Unexpectedly, she had slept so instantly and dreamlessly that it took her a while to remember where she was, in this white-painted bedroom, lying beneath the green floral-printed duvet.

Curiously, she slipped out of bed and went to look outside. She was at the back of the house, looking out on a well-tended but very French garden—not the English one of lawns and flowerbeds, but rows of vegetables and herbs and salad crops, protected by young fruit trees, and beyond, in the distance, the rooftops of Tarsac across the meadows.

Last night's darkness had lifted from her spirit. This was a magical place, and always had been, even in its erstwhile neglect, and every inch of it now attested to the love and care the new owner had lavished on it. Amber slipped into her new jeans and a silky shirt, and made her way downstairs to the kitchen, following the smell of brewing coffee.

Here she found a new and very different Luke, seated at the kitchen table, already surrounded by pages of manuscript and discarded coffee-cups—not the bitter, punitive individual of last night's exchanges, or the flippant, laughing man who had seized all opportunities to tease her in Westbury. Certainly not the reckless, moody, volatile spirit of those long ago days. This Luke was detached and cool and utterly professional, a writer at work, with little thought for anything else.

'I was beginning to think you'd sleep the clock round,' he said. 'Would you like to phone home before you have breakfast, then you can start work?'

Amber spoke briefly to Kate, then to Lucy, and was reassured by both of them that her daughter was well and happy. She had two cups of coffee and a croissant with jam, and then he showed her to a small room equipped as an office.

'You've used a word processor before, I presume?' he asked briskly. Amber looked at the sophisticated piece of equipment and nodded speechlessly. Westbury University was not yet kitted out with all this superior office technology, and he must have seen the machine she used there. But she told herself optimistically that any idiot who could type and read an instruction manual could use a word processor—she would manage somehow.

For the rest of the morning—once she had got to grips with the monster on her desk—Amber was in the dark heart of the Central African jungle with a band of harassed guerrilla fighters, beset by disease, communication problems and treachery. She pressed on steadily, fascinated by the unfolding story, and the interplay between the two main characters, a white mercenary and the black guerrilla leader, and did not break off until Luke went down to the village store and came back with more *charcuterie*.

'How are you getting on?' he asked, perching on the edge of her desk and dividing the food on to two plates.

'I'm half-way through chapter two,' she responded carefully.

'But you don't have an opinion?'

'I didn't know you were asking for one.' She paused. 'Well, you've got me hooked. I'd have to read on, even if I weren't typing it. This...this mercenary chap...he's not supposed to be you?'

'Tut, tut, Amber! As a writer yourself, you should know it doesn't work that way,' he chided her gently.

'But you did take part in a war like this,' she observed.

'I *reported* it,' he corrected. 'The only way I could do that was to live and move with the guerrillas, so I shouldered my assault rifle, even though I didn't know too much about how it worked, and went along for the ride. How's your novel coming along?' He switched topics abruptly.

Amber shrugged. 'Slowly. I can't compete in this league. I haven't done anything. My life has been so...circumscribed. Please don't say "write about what you know". I know so very little.'

He laughed, but there was no mockery in it.

'You know more than you think. I write this way because I make use of my journalistic experiences, but there are other ways...look at the torrid stuff the Brontës turned out, from a country parsonage! Liberate your imagination, Amber, and you'll speak with your own voice, and the authority of your years of living. But first you have to learn to let go a little.'

He leaned over and switched off the machine.

'Come with me. I want to show you something,' he said shortly.

Amber followed him outside, along a path through the vegetable garden and the orchard beyond, until they came to a stile with a field beyond, where a chestnut pony cropped the grass.

She looked curiously at Luke's unrevealing face as he called out softly and the pony trotted towards them, nuzzling their hands.

'He's sweet,' she said. 'Is he yours?'

'He is now,' he said drily, 'but if you look at him properly, Amber, you'll see he's far too small for me to ride.'

And then, as she looked at him, it dawned on her what he was saying, and she gasped, overcome by an emotion that was new to her where he was concerned. Remorse.

'You bought him for Kate to ride!' she cried. 'Oh, Luke, I ... I don't know what to say!'

'Don't say anything,' he cautioned her, his face still a mask. 'Just try—occasionally—to feel someone else's pain, as well as your own. Open up, Amber. There's a world out here, full of other human beings, who suffer the same way you do.'

He turned and walked back to the house, leaving her standing there alone and deeply disturbed. Luke had arranged for the pony to be there specifically to give Kate pleasure. He had probably looked forward to seeing her face, her ecstatic reaction when she saw him, just as Amber did when she put the parcels on Kate's bed on Christmas Eve ... all the Christmases and birthdays she'd been able to share with Kate, and he hadn't. He'd asked only for this one brief summer, a few short weeks, and she had thought herself so very smart, so quick-witted and clever, when she had deprived him of it.

She had hurt him, and just now he had allowed her to know it, to catch a glimpse of that hurt. It took a real man to do that, she admitted soberly, and all at once the resentment that had shored up her defences against him was no longer a strong enough barrier to hide behind.

She found him in the kitchen, making coffee.

'Luke,' she said, 'I'm sorry. Is there any way I can make it up?'

He shook his head, and there was no anger in him.

'As you said, it's probably too late,' he told her. 'Don't worry about the pony—I can always get someone from the village to groom and exercise him.'

But she hadn't only been talking about the pony. Open up, he had said, learn to feel another's pain. Had she ever? From the age of seventeen, she had been banking up the fires of resentment against him, so that they had never ceased to smoulder, even now. Why? Not, surely, because he had seduced her? She had gone to him willingly enough, she had to admit, if she looked back with unromantic honesty. But because, having taken her, she had not been enough for him. He had not loved her. That was his crime, and for that she was still making him pay, eleven years later.

Suddenly, she was looking at those far-off days, not through the filter of her heartbroken, youthful idealism, but with a stark, mature clarity of sight, as if coming back here had released a spring jammed shut for too long.

'He had an alarming tendency towards self-destruction,' Granville Stark had said, talking about Luke in those days, and Amber recalled him lecturing to the students at Westbury, looking back into a bleak, devastated area in his own psyche. '"I wake and feel the fell of dark..."'

He had been blighted, stunned by something, some experience, some knowledge, which had left him unable to love. Even Paula, who claimed to have known him so well, had failed to get through to him. Amber still did not know what it was that had scarred him so badly, but she knew it existed, as surely as she knew her own name.

He set down the coffee-pot.

'Amber,' he said, 'what's the matter? You look as if you've been struck by a thunderbolt.'

'Perhaps I have,' she whispered, and then, unable to face him in the raw, bright light of this new understanding, she turned and fled from him, ran headlong upstairs to her room and flung herself face-down on her bed, breathing heavily.

Minutes later she heard the door open softly, and felt the bed sag as he sat beside her, touching her shoulder with his hand.

'I didn't mean to upset you this badly,' he said quietly. 'I only wanted to make you think.'

'Oh, you did that, all right!' she muttered into the pillow. He'd made her think of him as a human being, capable of suffering, not a gossip-column figment of sexual scandal. And now she did not know how to cope with the end result of this revelation, for while she could attempt to feel scorn and disgust for the latter, the former stirred up deeper, more complex emotions.

Gently, he turned her over. Her eyes were huge in her pale face, lambent and bewildered, but they were no longer able to hide from the question in his. He smiled that slow, heart-wrenching smile, and the puzzle faded as her own smile answered it.

The room was very still and quiet, and the shutters she had left half closed to ward off the heat cast bars of golden-striped light across his body and her own.

And now she was aware of nothing beyond his actual physical presence beside her in the calm, variegated solitude of the room. She had waited eleven years for this moment, and it was here; she was not half-tipsy and confused, but undeniably sober and sure of what she was doing. It had to be. She could not go on living unless, once more, he made love to her.

His mouth on hers, the unhurried movement of his fingers unbuttoning her shirt were like an oasis in the desert to one who had known only mirages. There was nothing rushed or hasty about their loving, nothing fumbled or inept. She was scarcely aware of the shedding of their clothes, or the shedding of her years of inhibition. It all bore the measured, pulsating rhythm of a seductive dance, perfectly timed, each caress slowed down to give the ultimate, lingering pleasure. She explored and savoured every part of him, while offering him her body in its entirety, holding back nothing until she lay gasping and shuddering beneath him in exquisite release.

For a long while they did not speak. The experience had been too shatteringly sweet for words to do other than spoil it. They lay side by side, hip and shoulder touching, breathing deeply, copper hair and gold damply tangled on the pillow.

Only after some time had passed, Amber turned her head to one side and, looking into his eyes, said lightly but seriously, 'Please don't spoil it this time by apologising.'

He smiled.

'You're a very different woman now, Amber, and I'm a different man. But I didn't bring you here intending to make love to you, any more than I did then. It was . . . spontaneous, not calculated.'

With the new insight so painfully born that day, Amber looked back across the years and remembered something she had half forgotten, something that at the time she had scarcely given a thought.

'You had been dreaming,' she recalled. 'Something about Gemma...your wife? And a house collapsing.'

He didn't answer at first, and just for a moment she felt that dark past reaching out to reclaim him. Then he seemed to shake himself mentally.

'Yes,' he said. 'My wife, also a damn brilliant photographer. I took her with me to the Middle East to cover a meeting with the leader of one of the warring factions. A bomb planted by a rival faction exploded in the house while we were talking to him, and she was buried in the rubble.'

He brushed an impatient hand through the unruly hair flopping on his forehead.

'Silly idiot! She said, "I'm mortgaged up to my frillies for that equipment, I'm not leaving it behind!" I told her not to be so bloody daft, the place was falling down about our ears. Then a wall collapsed between us, and I don't remember any more until I woke up in the hospital. We'd been married for three weeks and two days.'

'Luke, that's awful! No wonder you had nightmares about it,' she said warmly. She thought, perhaps he woke up and thought I was Gemma ... or perhaps he neither knew nor cared who I was ... I was just a female body, comfort, solace ... and I thought I was the love of his life! But understanding had wiped out bitterness, and she could view it ruefully rather than accusingly.

'I wish,' she said, a trifle wistfully, 'you had explained that to me at the time.'

'I wish,' he echoed, 'that I could have spoken about it to *anyone* at the time. I couldn't. I was too busy blaming myself for having taken her to her death. It was a long time before I could see that she was only doing her job, as I was.'

He rolled over, traced a hand lightly over her hip, across the tautness of her stomach to the swelling eagerness of her breast.

'If I had been capable of explaining, would you have been mature enough to understand?' he asked shrewdly.

Amber was almost beyond the point where speech had any relevance, the touch of his hand was re-awakening the fires of sensuality, so that she wanted only to be taken all over again.

'I don't think...you even knew...who I was...' she gasped out.

Briefly, his caress was stilled.

'But I had reached the nadir—the lowest point,' he said soberly. 'I was on a hiding to oblivion, and very possibly you saved my life.' Drawing her to him again, he said, 'I know who you are *now*.'

That evening they had dinner at the Auberge du Pont. Madame, a little greyer and sparer, but otherwise unchanged, greeted Luke as an old friend, and kept glancing at Amber in puzzlement, as if she could not quite place her.

'That's not surprising. She only met you once, and while you're not easy to forget, you *have* changed some,' he grinned.

'Rubbish!' she retorted lightly. 'You probably bring so many women here, she can't tell one from another!'

A cloud crossed his forehead.

'I don't bring "women" here,' he said. 'This is the place I think of as home, far more than my London flat. It's my refuge, it's where I go when I want to work, or simply to recharge my batteries. It isn't a love-nest.'

Amber looked down at her plate of *escargots*; gripping a shell tightly, she made a great performance of withdrawing the snail with the special implement provided.

'I expect you've brought Paula here,' she said, with apparent casualness.

'Oh, yes, Paula, of course,' he said quite matter-of-factly, not troubling to deny it.

Of course. He and she were were having an affair, had spent most of the afternoon in bed together in extravagant abandonment, but that altered nothing. He desired her—that she could not doubt, but that was all.

Very carefully, in level, dispassionate tones, he spelled it out for her.

'A lot of the stuff you've probably read about me can be taken with a liberal sprinkling of salt,' he said. 'OK, I'm no angel... but I've neither the time nor the inclination for the rampant libertinism I'm credited with. It's true that after Gemma died I went a little wild where women were concerned. I didn't quite lay everything female that stood in my path, but... well, I had a good try. That was my reaction to what had happened, my way of dealing with it. These days, I'm a much quieter soul. I'm older, more reflective, ready for a steadier relationship.'

He looked at her quizzically, as if trying to figure out if she appreciated what he was trying to tell her. That he might have the odd fling... like this... but he had made a decision as to his future, and the woman with whom he would spend it.

'I quite understand,' she made herself say, very lightly. 'You're ready to settle down, whereas I need to break out and make up for lost time.' She even managed to laugh. 'I think you must be *my* wild oats, Luke!'

She was very quiet as they drove back to the farmhouse. Since they had met again this summer, she had been conscious of her desire for him, a constant ache which would not leave her. This afternoon he had more than satisfied that desire, but it had not stilled the ache, because it was rooted deeper than mere physical passion.

She no longer knew for certain whether what she had felt for him all those years ago was love, or whether it was girlish romanticism which personal disaster had turned sour. But this much she knew—she loved him now. With all her heart, body and soul she loved this man who was the father of her child, and would go on loving him. Doomed—she could not cast him out of her existence completely; because of Kate, she would have to see him, meet him, even when he was part of another woman's life.

He escorted her very politely and properly to the door of her room, and without a word other than 'goodnight' retired to his own. Amber undressed, got ready for bed, then stood in the centre of the room for a while, thinking soberly about what she was going to do. Then she slipped quietly along the corridor to his room and opened the door.

He was lying in bed, on his back, arms behind his head, but wide awake. The shutters were open, and moonlight revealed the muscles of his chest, rising and falling faintly with his breath. He neither spoke nor took his eyes off her as she let her nightdress fall to the floor about her feet and slid into bed, gasping with need as his skin touched hers.

She had gone to him consciously, in the full knowledge that he was about to commit himself to someone else, and if that was wrong, so be it, she would live with her conscience. While they were here alone he was hers, and if all she had was his desire, for as long as it lasted, then she would live with that, too.

The next three days Amber knew she would never forget. When they worked, they worked hard and with utter concentration—Luke wanted to press on before any more house guests turned up, and of necessity took up more of his time.

But they snatched hours off and drove around the peaceful, wooded countryside. They went to La Roque St Christophe, where neolithic dwellings honeycombed an entire cliff face, and they followed the guided tour up the precipitous stairways and narrow paths early man had hewn. Amber clutched Luke's arm, dizzy with vertigo as she looked down from the heights, convinced that her ancestors must have been far more agile and fearless.

Giving in to her pleas to return to ground level, he took her on to St Leon sur Vezere, where a lovely old church dreamed on a spur in the bend of the river, and to Montignac, where they sat near the graceful old bridge, watching the water flow strongly by. And finally to Domme, where they had first met, looking the same as it had on that memorable afternoon, in the hot summer sunshine.

'What a ninny I was then,' she said wryly as they paced the cobbled streets. She wasn't afraid of those old memories any more, for very soon she would have others, fresher and more painful. Very soon she would lose him for the second time.

'You were a sweet, lovely child on the threshold of womanhood,' he said, regarding her carefully. 'I forced you into a too-early flowering.'

She shrugged. 'What's past is past, Luke. Let's live in the present.'

At night, they made love with increasing passion, and the skill which came through their growing knowledge of one another. Amber was amazed by the variety of ways a man and a woman could give each other pleasure, and physically she held back nothing. But emotionally she kept it light, resisting a need to let him know how much she loved him.

He had been right about one thing—it was too late. She had come to love and respect him, and had overcome her reluctance to accept him as Kate's father, but for herself there was no real future involving him. He was the third party in what threatened to be quite an unpleasant divorce, with remarriage the only honourable outcome. Perhaps, as he had hinted, he would settle down and be reasonably faithful to Paula. I represent his last summer of freedom, she thought, and knew that their affair must end with these few days and nights of isolation. Once they were no longer alone together in the house, it would be over.

The telephone shrilled very early on the fourth morning, while Amber was in the kitchen making coffee.

'It's your turn,' he had told her, rolling over in bed and feigning sleep, and with a playful, affectionate slap on his rump she had slipped out of bed and gone downstairs.

Even with all those miles of wire and cable in between them, Paula's voice, demanding and faintly frantic, had the power to send shivers of ice down her back.

'I want to speak to Luke,' she said imperiously. 'This minute. Get him for me, will you?'

Amber clutched the robe at her middle as if Paula was somehow able to see that she was revealingly naked beneath it, her body still warm and glowing from his touch.

'I'm not sure if he's awake,' she said formally.

'Then wake him. This is urgent,' Paula commanded grimly, but looking round Amber saw him coming down the stairs, clad only in pyjama bottoms, running a hand through his thick, tousled hair. Her heart constricted with love and need, and holding out the receiver was like handing him over to the other woman, renouncing what small claim she might fool herself she had.

'It's Paula,' she said, retiring to the kitchen and busying herself with the coffee. She could hear his monosyllabic response to the lengthy tirade from the other end. 'All right... Yes... Calm down,' which told her almost nothing except that Paula was agitated, which she already knew. Then he said, 'We have to sort this out, once and for all. Don't do anything until I arrive.' And she had to put the coffee-pot down for fear her trembling hands would not be able to hold it. This was it—it was already over for her.

'I have to go to London,' he said, appearing in the doorway, looking suddenly tired and worn, for all that it was early morning. 'There are problems I can't take care of from here.'

'Is it . . . is it about the divorce?' Amber asked, reluctant but having to know.

'Yes,' was all he said in reply to that. 'There's a lot of work still to be done on the manuscript. Will you be all right here on your own for a few days?'

'Perfectly. Don't worry about it,' she said in a cool, practical voice. 'No problem.'

He took her hands, looked down very searchingly into her eyes.

'Amber,' he said. 'About you and me . . . and these last few days . . .'

Right now, when she was holding herself together so tightly that it hurt, the last thing she could face was another apology.

'Forget it, Luke,' she said curtly. 'You've a long journey ahead—you had better pack.'

# CHAPTER TEN

AMBER worked steadily through the day after he had gone, refusing to let herself think about anything else. Only at night, when she finally switched off the machine and went through the motions of cooking herself a meal, did the agony she had held at bay come flooding in.

They had been as close as a man and a woman could be during these days in France. But it hadn't meant anything to him, apart from the ephemeral pleasure of making love. Paula needed him and he had gone, left her—just like that.

Pouring herself a glass of wine, she wandered out on to the terrace. From here, the lights of the village were not visible, and apart from the stars the night was dense, black and uninhabited. But she wasn't afraid. The loneliness all around did not disturb her, it was peaceful and reassuring. The emptiness in her own heart was another matter. She stood for a moment gazing out into the intense silence of this serene heart of France, then turned, went inside, locked up and took herself to bed.

She had been at work for an hour or two the next morning when the telephone interrupted her. Probably Luke, phoning to ask how she was getting on with the work, she thought, and steeled herself to talk to him in a normal manner.

But it was Lucy's voice she heard.

'Now, Amber, I don't want you to panic,' her friend began warningly, and Amber's heart did a triple somersault of apprehension, her mother's instinct in no doubt as to the reason for this call.

'It's Kate, isn't it?' she demanded urgently. 'She's ill—something's happened to her! Tell me at once, Lucy!'

'She took a bad fall off Scarlet.' Lucy's voice was grave but steady. 'The horse cast a shoe and tripped, they were doing a fast canter at the time, and Kate went headlong over the reins. She was wearing her hat, of course, but she hit the ground pretty hard.'

Amber did not need to be told that she had not yet heard the worst. Oddly enough, she was deathly still and cold as she said, 'Tell me the rest, Lucy.'

'She's in Westbury General,' Lucy said. 'Concussion isn't surprising, but the thing is——' She hesitated, and Amber heard her fear fill the silence. 'Amber, this was hours ago, and she hasn't come round yet. I think you had better come home!'

This was the scene every mother rehearsed in her dreams, praying that it would never happen in reality. Her child was injured, seriously. Miles away, she lay in a coma...and she was not even there, at her side! Amber had heard those horror stories of people who remained locked in this half-life for months, linked to support systems that kept their bodies functioning while their minds floated in some mysterious limbo.

And yet, with all this horror racing through her mind, Amber moved in a suspension of frozen calm. She locked away Luke's manuscript, closed up the house and took the key to the Auberge du Pont, asking for it to be given to the regular caretaker, whom Amber did not know. From there, she ordered a taxi to take her to Périgueux, for the first time cursing the isolation of Luke's country retreat, and caught a fast train to Paris.

Amber had never travelled this distance on her own before, her French was rusty and everything and everywhere was strange to her. But she did not allow herself to be fazed by it; grimly she pressed on, asked her way, caught her connections, and finally got herself to the airport in time to catch the next available flight to Heathrow. Buckled into her seat for the first aeroplane journey of her life, she was still single-mindedly straining towards her destination, as if her determination could urge the jet to greater speed. She *had* to get to Kate. Nothing else mattered. What she would find when she got there, what she would do then, she could not permit herself to ask.

She arrived at Westbury in the golden calm of a summer evening, utterly exhausted but too strung up to realise it. There was no one to meet her at the station, since she could not have said what time she would get there, and she took a final taxi for the last lap of her agonised journey. Let her be all right, and then, let me be in time, the words repeated themselves ominously in her head, and she clenched and un-clenched her hands as they waited at every traffic light on the way to the hospital.

Lucy met her at the main entrance, and almost fell into her arms. Her refined features were contorted with worry, her usually immaculately groomed fair hair an uncombed mass around her shoulders.

'There's no change,' she said at once. 'She's stable, but still unconscious. Oh, Amber, I'm so sorry!'

Amber, sick with fear and almost fainting from fatigue and lack of food, found herself comforting her friend.

'Lucy—it wasn't your fault,' she insisted. 'Kate could have taken a tumble at any time, and neither you nor I could have prevented it. But I should have been here. I should never have left her.' She gripped Lucy's hand. 'I must go to her now. Poor love, she's all alone.'

'She's not alone, Amber,' Lucy said, keeping pace with Amber's fast stride along the antiseptic-scented corridors. 'Luke's here. He's been with her all day.'

Amber's pace checked.

*'Luke?'* she repeated uncomprehendingly. 'What's he doing here?'

'I think an angel sent him.' Lucy allowed herself a little smile as she took Amber's arm and they continued walking. 'I don't know how I'd have got through the day without him! He only phoned to have a word—just checking on your behalf that Kate was OK, he said, and thank heaven he did! He came straight here when I told him what had happened, and he's been here ever since.'

Amber's initial astonishment had faded into a numbed thankfulness. *She* should have been the one to sit by Kate's bedside and hold her hand, but since she could not, who better than Kate's father...the father she had never known? Maybe it was more, after all, than a biological accident. Maybe blood was a stronger link than anyone knew.

'He really cares about that child,' Lucy said, as if echoing her thoughts. 'The way he sat there, holding her hand...just as if she were his own. You owe him a real debt, Amber.'

Greater than you will ever know, Amber thought, as the sister ushered her into a private side ward.

Kate lay unmoving on the narrow bed, her head swathed in bandages, her small face so white that fear gripped Amber anew. Luke sat on a hard chair by the bed. His hair was ruffled and a shadow across his jaw proclaimed that he hadn't had time to shave, but he was talking softly and earnestly to the girl, as if in quiet conversation with her. He smiled, a tired but strength-giving smile as he caught sight of Amber, and got to his feet, his arm going instinctively round her shoulders.

Over her coppery head, he smiled sympathetically at Lucy.

'You look dead on your feet. Go and have a cup of tea and sit down.'

'I think I will,' she agreed. 'She has both of you now.'

After she had gone, Luke pulled up another chair, lowered Amber into it, and sat beside her.

'It isn't as bad as it looks,' he assured her quietly. 'She's breathing on her own, isn't connected up to a machine. It's just that she hasn't regained consciousness. The doctor said there's no way of telling, it could be any minute, or several hours.'

Or never? Amber looked down at the still form, and her hand gripped Luke's convulsively.

'You...you spoke to the doctor?' she asked faintly.

'I had to. Lucy was going frantic, they wouldn't tell her anything, just kept saying they had to wait until her mother arrived. So I sort of muscled in and told him I was Kate's father. I think Lucy must have twigged, Amber—they only talk to next of kin as a rule.'

She gave a wan smile.

'It doesn't matter now, Luke. I'm just glad you were here.' Her troubled eyes sought his. 'When I came in, just now ... you were talking to Kate?'

He shrugged, discomfited by emotion, a rare occurrence for him.

'No one knows, for sure, just how much gets through to them in that state,' he said. 'I reckoned it couldn't harm, and you know I like the sound of my own voice.' He forced a grin and held her hand more tightly. 'Don't you dare give up, Amber. She's going to make it. We'll pull her through, between the two of us.'

They sat by her bedside until it grew dark. Amber talked. She talked about everyday, unimportant things, she delved back into Kate's early years, dredging up funny little incidents and sayings, she talked about horses and riding ... and somehow she found herself talking about the Perigordian farmhouse and the chestnut pony in the field behind it.

'He's so gorgeous, I wish you could have seen him,' she finished lamely, sinking into a deep hopelessness as Kate showed no sign of responding.

'But you will see him, Kate,' Luke's voice broke in confidently. 'He's still there, waiting, and when you're better your Mum and I will take you out there.'

Amber looked up slowly, meeting his gaze, and a flicker of anger stirred her numbness.

'A promise to an unconscious child is still a promise, Luke,' she told him soberly. 'Don't make them if you won't be in a position to keep them.'

The spark ignited, and the blue eyes flashed fire at her.

'Give me one good reason why I shouldn't be?'

'Paula—you were supposed to be meeting her today,' she reminded him dully.

'Paula can wait!' he snapped brusquely. 'What the hell has her wretched divorce to do with you, me or our child?'

Amber's mouth fell open. *Everything*, she wanted to retort, since she'll be with you, and if I know anything, she won't want a convalescent ten-year-old queering her pitch!

'For pete's sake, Luke——' she began furiously, then checked herself. Here, in a hospital ward, over a sick child's bed, they were aruging, for all the world like a frantically worried married couple...like parents! They stared at each other in wry amazement, and suddenly a small movement seized their attention. Kate stirred, coughed, and her eyes flickered open, moving dazedly in her pale face from one to the other of the angry adults at her side.

Amber was crying, copious but silent tears running down her face unchecked, her daughter's hand caught between both hers, while Luke leapt to his feet, opened the door and bawled imperiously, *'Nurse!'* Then, kneeling at Amber's side, he drew her head to his shoulder.

'I told you we'd do it—between us!' he said.

Amber was often to wonder afterwards if the sound of their voices raised in sharp argument had been the lifeline, dropped into those mysterious depths, that hauled Kate back to consciousness where all their soft talk had failed to elicit a response. There was no way of knowing for sure, but she was awake, and complaining of aches and pains everywhere.

'Not surprising, after the fall you took, young lady!'
Lucy, quickly summoned to hear the good news, was
almost laughing with relief.

It was some time before the doctor finished his examination and announced that he could see no reason
why the patient should not now make steady progress
towards recovery. Lucy had gone home a little earlier,
but Amber and Luke sat by Kate until she subsided
into a natural sleep, when the nurse suggested gently
that they should go and get some rest themselves.

Only then did Amber realise how utterly, bone-
wearily exhausted she was, and hungry, too—she had
eaten virtually nothing since that morning.

Luke took one look at her, propelled her towards
the Jaguar, and almost lifted her into the front passenger seat. Then he drove to the only place in
Westbury that was still open and serving food at this
late hour—the Chinese takeaway shop. Too tired to
question, almost too tired to care what he did next,
Amber nursed the hot foil packs all the way to her
cottage.

And so she came to be curled up in a corner of the
sofa eating sweet and sour pork and crispy pancake
rolls, with Luke Tremayne sprawled on the floor at
her feet. She had not expected to be with him again,
except formally, in the company of others, and knew
he should really be somewhere else tonight. But she
didn't dwell on that too minutely. She didn't have the
energy, nor did she want at this moment to burden
herself further with anything unpleasant. Kate was
going to be all right, and Luke was here with her. For
tonight, it was enough.

He cleared away the foil and paper wrappings, and
made coffee. Tiger stalked in, purring, and jumped

on Amber's lap, where he settled contentedly. Kate had been coming in every day to feed him; he could not understand why she had missed him today, and had been ecstatic to see them. Amber's hand, stroking the short, thick fur moved ever more slowly, her head began to droop, and without any warning sleep overtook her.

She awoke in her own bed, and at first could not place herself. Hadn't she gone to sleep last night in the green and white bedroom at the farmhouse? What was she doing here, and how had she made the transition? And then she remembered Kate and the hospital, the mad dash across France, and the Chinese supper with Luke. But she did not recall climbing the stairs to the bedroom. He must have put her to bed—once again!

Her clothes were neatly folded over a chair, and she discovered that she had slept in her bra and pants. He must have undressed her, without her even knowing. Amber thought of all the other times, over the days they had spent in France, when he had slowly and lingeringly divested her of her clothes, deliberately extending and prolonging the pleasure, and hot colour rushed to her face at the memory.

The door opened, and she looked up to see him entering, carrying a tray with a coffee-pot and cups.

'I didn't want to disturb you too much last night—you looked pretty far gone, so I just made you as comfortable as I could,' he said. 'Why are you blushing, Amber? I've seen you wearing less than that many times.'

'Please——' she said distractedly.

He set down the tray and poured the coffee.

'I know, you prefer not to think about it now, right?' he said coolly. 'The wild oat season is over and done with. Before you ask——' the change of subject was abrupt and typical '——I've already phoned the hospital, and Kate is fine. She was sitting up and demanding breakfast. I'll run you over to see her when we've done the same.'

Amber sipped her coffee thoughtfully. She would have liked to continue with this happy pretence of normality—Mum and Dad having breakfast together, then driving over to see their daughter, but it was an illusion, and she had to stop believing it.

'Luke, you've been wonderful, but I know you've got other matters to...to attend to in London. Shouldn't you be on your way? I can manage now I know Kate's going to be all right, truly I can.'

He slammed the cup down so hard that the china on the tray rattled in frantic unison.

'Damn you, Amber, stop trying to shut me out!' he exploded furiously. 'You've made it more than clear to me where I stand, and I know I can't compete with your idyll of a marriage, but Kate is still *my* child, whether you like it or not!'

Leaving her staring after him in utter astonishment, he strode out of the bedroom, banging the door with such violence that every window-frame in the cottage shook with the impact.

Amber scrambled swiftly out of bed, shrugged on an old dressing-gown she left pegged behind the door, and sped barefoot after him, following the reverberations of his angry footsteps. She found him in the kitchen, back rigidly turned to her, shoulders hunched, staring blankly out of the window.

'Just hang on a minute!' she accosted him. '*You* were the one with the idyllic marriage, as I remember! The one so grief-stricken he was drinking himself to oblivion and making love to women he didn't know from Eve!'

He whirled round then, facing her, and she caught her breath at the naked honesty in his eyes.

'Is that what you think? Do you want the truth— the real truth, not the soap-opera version invented by the Press? That was no idyll—it was a shooting match! We argued all the time, tore each other to shreds! It was like a drug—we couldn't leave each other alone, but we did each other no good. Getting married was a crazy, impulsive, lunatic——' He paused, drew a deep breath. 'We were in Venice. She said I was a no-good wastrel, and if I were a man, I'd make an honest woman of her. I said I was going back to the Middle East, and if she were my wife, I'd expect her to come along. The mad female called my bluff. She said I needed a photographer, and she was the best I'd get. That much was true, anyhow!'

Some of the tension drained out of him, as he said more quietly, 'It was the guilt that was destroying me, Amber, as I told you at the farmhouse. But not because I'd loved her. That wasn't love. Love is——' Again he paused, searching for the reality behind the abstraction. 'Love is what kept me at the hospital all yesterday, chewing my fingernails clean up to my elbows! And what made me sleep on your sofa last night, putting up with being walked all over by a heavy-footed cat! It's what we shared at the farm-house, working and living together, and yes—making love the way we did. And don't tell me that was just sex, because it wasn't—not for me! Love is what I feel for that kid at the hospital—and her mother!'

He crushed Amber fiercely into his embrace, holding her to him so tightly that she feared he would break her ribs, kissing her face and her throat over and over again. She struggled dementedly, beating her fists against his chest, fighting a desperate battle against him and her own overwhelming desire to give in, and be swept along on a tide of passion.

'Luke, Luke, stop it! I can't take any more of this!' she cried, twisting in his arms and finally breaking free only because he sensed the force of her desperation, and let her go. She drew back from him, and they stared at each other like two wounded animals, wary of provoking any further hurt.

'You can't love two women—not if *I'm* one of them!' she told him. 'I can't share you with Paula, and you told me in so many words at the farmhouse that you were planning to settle down with her!'

He sighed, lifted his hands as if about to shake her, then let them fall to his side.

'With *you*, my dear, crazy, furiously independent girl, not with *her*!' he said exasperatedly. 'Maybe I wasn't capable of loving you when we first met, but you represented a turning point in my life. I picked up the pieces, got them together, and went forward. And I knew very shortly after I met you again that you were the one for me—even before I realised Kate was my child. That's why I took you to France. I had to hang on to you, to persuade you to live in the present, with me, not in the past, with Lawrence.'

His hands found hers. They could no longer keep from touching each other, and Amber did not see how

she could bring herself to let him go now, knowing
that he loved her.

'Lawrence wasn't the past I couldn't forget—*you*
were,' she told him soberly. 'He was good to me, and
to Kate, but I never really loved him, and he knew it.
I married him because he was there when I needed
someone, and I couldn't have you. So I had my share
of guilt to live with, believe me.'

She leaned her head against his shoulder.

'But we'll only be taking on more guilt, Luke, don't
you see? There's Paula—she's loved you for so long,
and now there's the divorce——'

He silenced her by covering her mouth briefly with
his hand.

'Amber, if you love me, you've got to trust me and
believe I'm telling the truth when I say, quite em-
phatically, that Paula and I were never, ever lovers.
*Never,*' he repeated firmly, seeing the flash of incre-
dulity in her eyes. 'Oh, I admit that there were times
when we might have been, when we came close, but
I always avoided the final step along that path. For
one thing, she's my editor, a good one, and business
and pleasure are best kept apart. And an obsessive
passion like hers scares me—do you think I'd tie
myself to it for life?'

'Then how come you're involved in her divorce?'
she questioned him, still puzzled. 'You dashed over
here like a bat out of hell when she phoned, to "sort
out things, once and for all".'

'I'm not involved in it, and if she led you to believe
I was, she's lying,' he stated categorically. 'I don't
think there is a third party concerned, but somehow,
Malcolm thinks—or she has allowed him to think—
that there is, and that it's me. She stayed that night

at the river house, remember? But Granville and Clarissa were there, too, and nothing happened. And when she came down to see me that weekend, to tell me she was getting a divorce, I saw what she had in mind and pointed her in the direction of London before teatime! I'm not going to be manipulated into the position of co-respondent when, for once in my life, I'm totally innocent.'

The rakish grin she knew so well spread across his face, lightening his features, and he touched the tip of her nose with his finger.

'Your Honour, I swear I never touched her!' he half joked, and then, more seriously, said, 'I have to see Malcolm, and convince him of that. Once he's sure she hasn't been unfaithful to him, there's a chance he'll halt the proceedings and there'll be a reconciliation. I don't think Paula really wants a divorce—unless there's a remarriage at the end of it.'

Amber melted into his arms, and for a while all else was forgotten. She had travelled a long, perilous road from the sun-bleached square in Domme, where she had first fallen in love, and never dared to believe that Luke would ever be hers. But some part of her had always waited for him, and at last, here he was, truly loving her.

'Why don't you tell Malcolm you're engaged?' she murmured wickedly. 'That's the only way you'll persuade him you don't have designs on his wife, although I'll hold you to it, of course—you'll have to marry me!'

His smile caught hold of her heart, making it turn over with a happiness so fierce that it was very nearly pain.

'You just try getting yourself out of it, lady!' he said. 'Let me tell you the way it's going to be. First, we go and see our daughter. As soon as she's fit to leave hospital, we'll bring her home, here, and arrange the wedding. Then we'll all go back to France together.'

His voice was more serious than she had ever heard it, as he continued, 'One day, when we think she's old enough to understand, we'll tell her the truth about us, about herself—without detracting anything from the part Lawrence played in her life. But that's a decision we'll take together. We're not alone any more, Amber. You'll always have me, and I'll always have you.'

He swung her up into his arms, and she saw a mischievous but quite determined twinkle return to the blue eyes.

'But first of all, we're going right back to bed. I take it you don't have any objections?'

'How can I say no?' she asked, winding her arms around his neck. 'You're a hard habit to break, Luke. I might just as well give up trying!'

# HARLEQUIN
## *Romance*®

## Coming Next Month

**#3049 ANOTHER TIME, ANOTHER LOVE Anne Beaumont**
Laurel Curtis isn't planning to change her status as a single mother. A
traumatic experience with one man was enough. Connor Dyson, an Australian
property tycoon buying the lease on her flat, has other ideas—like taking over
Laurel, too!

**#3050 PARTNERS IN PASSION Rosemary Carter**
Teri comes back to her grandfather's African game farm where eight years
ago, before she had to move with her parents, she had loved Rafe—and
thought he loved her, too. Now Rafe greets her as a stranger.

**#3051 FACE VALUE Rosemary Hammond**
Christine agrees to do one last modeling job before she changes careers. John
Falconer, however, has devised the assignment of a commercial for his
company simply to meet her—and he offers Chris another proposition entirely.

**#3052 HOME FOR LOVE Ellen James**
When interior designer Kate Melrose is hired to redecorate an unknown
client's home, she falls instantly in love—with the house! But she soon falls
even harder for its owner, the handsome, irascible Steven Reid.

**#3053 THE CHAIN OF DESTINY Betty Neels**
When Guy Bowers-Bentinck comes to her rescue, Suzannah, alone in the
world and without a job, is forced to accept his help. Not that she wants to be
beholden to such an infuriatingly arrogant man!

**#3054 RASH CONTRACT Angela Wells**
Karis doesn't welcome the reappearance of Nik Christianides in her life—
reawakening tragic memories she's spent years trying to suppress. Now,
though, she has to listen to him because he has a way of replacing what she
had lost.

**In April, Harlequin brings you the
world's most popular romance author**

# JANET DAILEY

## *No Quarter Asked*

**Out of print since 1974!**

After the tragic death of her father, Stacy's world is shattered. She needs to get away by herself to sort things out. She leaves behind her boyfriend, Carter Price, who wants to marry her. However, as soon as she arrives at her rented cabin in Texas, Cord Harris, owner of a large ranch, seems determined to get her to leave. When Stacy has a fall and is injured, Cord reluctantly takes her to his own ranch. Unknown to Stacy, Carter's father has written to Cord and asked him to keep an eye on Stacy and try to convince her to return home. After a few weeks there, in spite of Cord's hateful treatment that involves her working as a ranch hand and the return of Lydia, his ex-fiancée, by the time Carter comes to escort her back, Stacy knows that she is in love with Cord and doesn't want to go.

**Watch for *Fiesta San Antonio* in July and
*For Bitter or Worse* in September.**

JDA-1